Bald Spots
and Blue Suits

Bald Spots
& Blue Suits

Modern Fables

Henry Henkel

Other Islands Press

OTHER ISLANDS PRESS
128 South Mill Road, Princeton Junction, NJ 08550

Library of Congress catalog data available upon request.
Library of Congress Control Number: 2010940035

Designed by Tony Meisel

Printed in the United States of America
Hardcover EAN: 978-0-9749733-4-0
Trade paperback EAN: 978-0-9749733-8-8
eBook EAN: 978-0-974-9733-7-1

10 9 8 7 6 5 4 3 2 1

To my wife, Katherine, and my children: Katie, Dani, Joe, and Anna—for their unwavering love and support.

To my sister Kathleen, I don't know where I would be without all that she has done for me.

Contents

Bald Spots and Blue Suits • 1

9/11/2001: The Tear That Refused to Fall • 33

Visto's Church: An Apologue • 53

Cinderella Has Cellulite • 65

Hazen's Notch • 79

The Gathering Tree • 101

Lone Wolf • 121

Connecting Thoughts • 135

Lost Sailor • 175

Song for the Wretched • 189

Bald Spots and Blue Suits

John was screaming into the phone now. "You're saying that my pitch is bad? I live on Main Street and I die on Broadway? That's where you are wrong, Jake. I can make it on Broadway. I can handle big city clients. I need to make it there. That's where the money is. I'll fold up and die trying to live on Main Street and in small towns. You don't know what you are talking about. Give me a chance, goddamn it."

The room went silent for a moment and then...

"Well, it's obvious to me that you just don't give a damn." John slammed the receiver into its cradle. He stood for a moment, seething, trying to control his rage. He could find nothing in the room to which he could direct his focus. Then, John saw the door to his balcony. He grasped the faux brass knob, pulled the door open, and stepped out.

The November trees were meaningless beings far from the bloom of spring, their bark dark and wet. Beyond them lay the city of St. Louis, a soft center of light in the distance, diffused by the rain and the dampness of the day. The highway, which ran near Clayton, completed John's vista. Speeding lumps of cold, wet steel were sliding along a ribbon of concrete leading somewhere fast and then stopping.

Looking down at the balcony, John thought, "Jesus Christ, what is this thing?" He was standing on a rectangular ledge no more than three feet wide and five feet long. Looking to either side of him, he noticed that all the rooms in the hotel had double French doors that led to microscopic balconies. The sheer inanity of the situation had momentarily directed his anger away from his job. The strange attraction that small towns like Clayton had once held for John had long since disappeared. John found irony and cynicism in a place he would have found to be oddly quaint in the past.

"Who wants to be in Clayton, Missouri?" John shouted to no one in particular. He scrubbed his face with his right hand and muttered to himself. This town was just another pit in a series of pits in which he spent his life and made his money.

John had forgotten that it was raining when he first stepped onto the ledge. It was starting to pour now. He went inside, closed the door, and locked it with the absentminded efficiency of one who travels too often.

As he shook the water off his body, John wondered

why they had bothered to put a lock on a door inacces-
sible to all save the birds. Then he admonished himself for
locking the door. John was having a bad day with John.
It wasn't always that way; it just seemed that lately he was
having more bad days than good. John shook his head in
disgust. He sat in the faux cherry chair behind the faux
cherry desk beneath a print of some unnamed artist's trib-
ute to mediocrity. Across the room hung another print of
a steam locomotive barreling through a tree-covered vale
on its way to somewhere fast and then stopping. Who
picks out the art for hotel walls anyway? wondered John.

He looked at his wrinkled, freckled hands. It had
been a long time. He had been selling on the road for
what seemed to be an eternity. Two divorces and three
kids later, he was alone in a room in Clayton, Missouri,
and it was raining. The trivial nature of his sales job was
problem enough for John. To realize that there was not
another person who truly cared about him and his life's
work sometimes became too much to take. Still, he had
associates and friends with whom he could always laugh
and make jokes and with whom he rehashed the same
sleepy stories about nothing that were the fabric of his
past. Did anything really matter?

Thanksgiving was coming and then there would be
Christmas, and then another goddamn year. What else
could he do? He had no reason to stop. He had no reason to go on. He was tired and he was depressed and he

needed to get out of himself. He needed to get out.

He realized that his thoughts were morphing into "pop psych" babble, and it annoyed him. Still, there were times when he wondered if he'd ever commit suicide. He felt that most people killed themselves because they lost, or never established, a connection with something real and important in their lives. John was the antithesis of this thought pattern. He always told his friends to shoot him if he ever became like the "real worlders" that he encountered every day. Like the accoutrements of his hotel room which validated his view of the world around him as a jumbled collection of the curiously mediocre, John's life and belief system functioned best when he thought of the world as a toy placed before him for his benefit. All life's experiences, all life's arguments and struggles needed to be somehow unreal and not pertinent to him in order for John to accept them.

John was a man of convenient cynicism. He paused to look at himself in the mirror. He had too many wrinkles in his ill-fitting suit, on his body, and in his life. Never happy with the reflection he saw in the mirror, John thought it might be time to change his focus. He decided it was time to walk the streets of Clayton and find some dinner.

The rain had stopped. The streets were wet and deserted. John walked away from the hotel and into the darkness that was the heart of Clayton. It was November, and the town was already decorated for Christmas. This brought some joy to John, as Christmas was always an especially happy time of the year for him. Business was less hectic, people were out and in generally good moods, and he enjoyed shopping for odd and special gifts for the uncaring few he had dubbed his closest friends. His mood brightened as he walked the dark and empty streets of Clayton.

John had never been to Clayton before. It was his standard practice in a new city to let his body wander aimlessly until he felt that he had found a spot suitable for his mind to settle. While he sometimes searched for function, and sometimes searched for style, he was always looking for something new and different. John was always looking for the place, the face, the situation that could lead to happiness or surprise. In some places and in some spaces, he felt like he was diving into small waves of inadequate water. As he walked the streets of Clayton, he noticed how quiet it was. He could hear his own footfalls on the damp sidewalk. In New Orleans, one's feet were moved to dance. In New York, the noise of a footfall was drowned out by the action. In Clayton, one could hear everything. The noise had an odd effect on John. This town was too quiet. He began to get annoyed.

If I don't find a place to sit soon, he thought, I'll go out of my mind. It was then that he noticed that he was outside of City Hall. Just beyond the building, there was a park of small trees and brick, bushes and concrete benches, with a bronze statue erected to the memory of the town's first mayor. The park was decorated for Christmas.

Every branch of every tree was strung with lights of gold, red, and green. There was a large wooden Nativity with real straw and life-size figures of Christ, Joseph, and Mary. The bronze mayor wore a beautiful Christmas wreath around his neck as a yoke might be tossed upon an ox. The sight was overwhelming in this damp community of bare trees and empty streets. No one, save John, was there to appreciate the sight, a beacon of joy and celebration in this otherwise lifeless town. John sat for a moment on a cold, gray bench and wondered how much time and money it cost the taxpayers to put up and take down all these decorations every year.

It was then that John began to consider the town, what he'd seen and where he'd been. The town of Clayton, Missouri, had a certain Jeffersonian symmetry about it, though it lacked creativity and imagination. Every street and every building seemed to be balanced one against the other. Each street was perfectly straight, and they all met at perfectly perpendicular angles with crosswalk signs set back on an equidistant basis throughout the town. This place was too clean, too uncomplicated, too homogenized for creative thought. This was a town constructed by people with money but no imagination—people who understood convenience but not lasting beauty. Burnished mediocrity always annoyed John, perhaps because it reminded him of whom he was and what he had become, perhaps because it reminded him of everyone he had ever dealt with in his life.

This was also a town concerned with a satisfied stomach. There were more restaurants per square foot in Clayton than John had ever seen in his life. Storefront Thai, beside storefront Indian, beside storefront Mexican, next to a pizzeria that was beside an Irish bar and down the street from a Midwestern version of Central American delicacies. John was overwhelmed by the number of choices he had, but skeptical about their authenticity. In the end, John finally decided on Mad Mike's Irish Pub because he figured that Irish food was so bad he couldn't go far wrong, and that, at least, the drinking should be good at a place called Mad Mike's.

He opened the door to a smoky bar. The smell of cigarettes almost choked him as he walked in. His steady brown eyes surveyed the situation as he struggled to find a place to sit. Neither his mood nor the town would permit challenge tonight. John sat in the first seat he saw on the "L," or short, side of the bar. John was never much interested in sitting at the long end of the bar unless he was with some friends. From the short side, one could see everything. From the long side, it was too evident that you were alone. John ordered a beer and some shepherd's pie: How badly could a dump like this screw up mashed potatoes and leftover ground beef?

A marginally overweight woman was sitting at the bar with two friends smoking cigarettes and drinking mixed drinks. The women appeared to be watching a ball game about which they seemed to know nothing and care little, yet they periodically asked the bartender for updates so, John theorized, they could look smart when their dates arrived. The overweight woman whom John had noticed first had a gravelly voice that could only have developed from a lifelong relationship with a cigarette.

In a rather short time, John watched her down three tumblers of scotch. By the time she had finished the third, her attention was wavering. She seemed to be weaving between trying to focus on the game and the conversation of her friends. She stared off into space and had the vacant look of a person who had served herself too many drinks at too fast a pace. John wondered if there were visions of sugarplums or other sweet things dancing in her head. He chuckled at his own delicious insensitivity. A salesman who doesn't like people is not as silly as it seems, he thought. He ordered another beer, and his gaze was redirected to a far more appealing woman who was also in the bar.

Her shoes were elegant and stylish. From a distance, she looked to have a delicately formed face that was worthy of his attention. Her hair was long, blonde, and silky, extending halfway down her back in one beautiful sheath that moved as gracefully as she did. She wore a sheer black dress that was elegant beyond the room, providing greater insight into what John thought might be a perfect female form. For some inexplicable reason, his glance fell directly upon her hands, which were gently folded on the table before her. They were framed in the light from a recessed ceiling fixture that had a few cobwebs spun across it. There was a pale grace about them that, to John, revealed an inner peace and goodness rarely recognized in the world.

As the barmaid placed the woman's dinner before her, she removed a green napkin from the table and laid it on her lap. It did not surprise John one bit that this woman silently made the sign of the cross in a public place before beginning to eat the meal placed before her. She closed her eyes and said what John imagined to be a short prayer.

The fixture above and behind her head provided a perfect backlight for her profile, making her seem angelic. A hazy golden aura surrounded her silken hair and her flawless pale skin. When she closed her eyes, the lids seemed to move slightly as her conscious thought must have moved to dreams. John could imagine the visions of peaceful places and soft tones that drifted through her perfect body and beautiful mind. If fear existed, it was not from deeply rooted dragons or vines of despair. Perhaps those hands instinctively recoiled from civilization's dirt and hypocrisy and so remained pale and graceful.

John thought this to be a strong woman who could very well be aware of the tricks and cynicism of the world without ever expressing a word to condemn it. Still, hers was a face so beautiful that it somehow drove one's attention to the resolute peacefulness contained in those hands. How does one achieve such grace and purity in a world filled with despicable people? John wondered.

"Excuse me, how'd you like to help me finish my crosswords?" John's reverie was interrupted by a tanned woman who was wearing what appeared to be beaver skin pants that clung to her body too tightly. "You know the crosswords?" She waved her book in his face.

"Oh…yeah, sure." Normally, John would have jumped at so accessible an invitation from a reasonably pretty woman, but his mind was still preoccupied. For a time, he helped the woman with the tightly wrapped pants. But an occasional furtive glance always returned to the woman in the black dress. The last time he looked, the woman in black noticed him and briefly smiled in his direction.

She moved her right hand slightly and adjusted what appeared to be a thick green rubber band on her left wrist. Then she pulled on what John saw to be another thick green rubber band on her right wrist. It was as though she was trying to give her wrists a breath of fresh air in the dim lights and dark smoke of this dank and low-class bar.

John looked at the woman on his right, who was feverishly flipping through the back pages of her cross-word book, searching for the answers to her puzzle. John couldn't believe that she had resorted to cheating so quickly. He wondered why she bothered. What joy was there in copying the answers into the blank squares? Or, could it possibly be that this was her way to approach men in a bar?

John ordered one more beer and tried to summon up the courage to speak to the woman in black. While he drank, he watched her eat. He tried to capture the essence of every movement of this woman who, with her pure and graceful hands, had pushed everything else out of this bar and out of his thoughts. Her small and graceful mannerisms captured his attention. Her body was so deli-cately balanced that a certain tilt to her head forced a cor-responding movement in her hair that kept every element of her being in a perfect frame, a vision of magnificent elegance and simple perfection.

The crossword lady's nose was deep into the answer section trying to ferret out the solution to a particularly vexing clue. John felt no need to excuse himself from her; this was Mad Mike's after all. He focused his attention on ginning up the courage to approach the lady with the perfect hands.

John moved toward the table with caution and an aura of shyness that was odd for a man of his age and experience. The woman in black had just finished eating. Delicately, she dabbed at the corners of her mouth. Her manner of style caught John by surprise. What was she doing in this bar? She noticed John when he was about five feet away—too far to ask a question, too close to deny he was doing anything other than approaching her.

"What's a nice girl like you doing in a place like this?" John had worked this line before. It was his contention that a corny opening got past an awful lot of the uneasiness involved in a first encounter with anyone. It also gave the other person an opportunity to be straight, funny, or both, thereby providing insights into their personality that might have otherwise taken many drinks and many hours to discover.

She smiled a simple knowing smile and replied, "I am waiting for a friend…a girlfriend." Her smile broadened as she emphasized the last word in her statement as a playful response to John's awkward approach.

Her voice was different than John had expected. Instead of a delicate lilt, it had a deeper tonal quality. It was neither manly nor angelic, just…unexpected.

"Oh…well…if you are meeting someone, maybe I should just move on."

The woman smiled more broadly and motioned to the empty chair beside her. "Come. Sit down. Let's talk. My friend is late, and honestly, I don't want to be seated alone in this bar for very long. Most of the people here seem kind of old and creepy to me. There doesn't seem to be a whole lot of meaningful discussion going on around here. I'm guessing that most everybody is just looking for someone to go home with tonight."

John smiled at the lady in black and sat down. He was instantly impressed by the direct nature of her conversation. Her eyes did not waver, her glance did not stray, as she spoke to him about the bar and its patrons. This level of direct conversation was always appreciated by John. In his life at work, and even his life at home, people rarely said what they meant. They offered some semblance of their feelings, but rarely the full story. This often led to confusion and frustration for John. He always asked that people just say what they meant; he had finally found a woman willing to do so in Clayton, Missouri.

She held out one of those beautiful hands in a manner appropriate to its grace. "By the way, my name is Mary." Pale Mary, John thought, as she shook his hand. It was one of the most gentle handshakes he had ever received.

"I'm John. I'm just passing through myself. Here on business. What about you?"

"I flew in yesterday for my grandmom's funeral, which was this morning. I'm here to meet an old high school girlfriend tonight. I fly out tomorrow afternoon."

John was amazed. "You went to high school in this town? It looks too new, too clean, too neat to have any kids in it."

Mary laughed. "I never said I went to school here. I am meeting a friend from school who happens to live here. I haven't seen her in about five years. You wouldn't catch me dead in this town, yet death is what's caught me here. My grandmom loved it. The restaurants, the quiet neatness of it all, really appealed to her. Unfortunately, it doesn't appeal to me."

John smiled. "So glad to hear you don't like this place much either. It is way too antiseptic for me. Where do you live now?"

Mary was about to answer as the bar door opened and a masculine-looking woman walked in. Her pants were too short, her shirt clung tightly to large breasts that rested on an ample stomach, and her slipperlike shoes were water-stained.

Mary leapt from the table in the middle of John's question. "Lisa, how are you? I've missed you so." The two women almost crushed each other in an overenthusiastic embrace that was noticed by the entire bar. They then kissed each other on the cheek and hugged again.

John was crestfallen. This was the high school friend? If that was true, his night was over. The instant attraction he felt to Mary was now going to be trumped by the presence of an old friend. John needed to find a graceful exit from the situation. It seemed slightly odd to him that the fact that he needed to leave caused him to feel a bit upset. He loved the way Mary said grandmom instead of grandma or grandmother; it seemed so grounded and real. As he thought these things, Mary introduced Lisa. Lisa extended her stubby little hand and squeezed John's too tightly as she said hello.

John greeted Lisa and grabbed his drink off the table as the women sat down to talk. For a split second, he stood between them, not sure about what he should do next. Uncomfortable and awkward, John made an abrupt waving motion with his right hand, attempting a silent good-bye to Mary.

John thought that Mary looked a bit forlorn, a bit disappointed about his departure. She interrupted Lisa's excited squeals to approach him. She smiled the most beautiful smile John had ever seen and looked directly at him with steady blue eyes. "I'm from New York City."

She whispered, "I need to spend some time with my friend. We made plans. Don't you dare leave this bar before she does, because I would like to speak with you before I go." She patted him on the arm. "We'll talk later."

Lisa's eyes widened and rolled toward John as Mary returned to the table. "Who is he? What's going on? You've got to tell me."

Mary's eyes avoided Lisa's as she looked down at the table. "There's nothing to tell. We just met. There's just something about him I really like. Let's talk about you. How's the family? Do you have pictures?"

John returned to his seat on the bar's short side, where

the lady in the beaver skin pants was busily cheating on her second crossword. He ordered a drink as his gaze returned to Mary. The friend was prattling on about a stack of pictures before her. Mary's eyes caught John's, and she smiled slightly as she first pretended to listen to Lisa's endless stories about nothing, and then returned her full attention to Lisa.

John was as happy and confused as he'd ever been in his life. He took a deep draught of the drink before him and tried to make sense of it all. He was tremendously excited about what had just happened, but he didn't know how it had happened. What was he going to do now? He wanted to just sit and watch Mary, but that seemed inappropriate and creepy. He knew that the Mistress of the Crosswords was going to bother him again any minute. While he wanted to help and flirt because it gave him something to do, he didn't want to risk losing Mary's invitation to speak with her again. On the other hand, he didn't even know her or understand her intentions. Why should he care? Wasn't one in the hand worth two in the bush?

He finished his drink and then ordered another. Mentally, he reminded himself not to get too drunk. Suddenly, his forearm was slapped. "I need a five-letter word for 'cheater.' Got any ideas, big boy?" Her smile was inebriated, flirtatious, and vacuous all at once. She rolled her tongue across her front teeth salaciously. "Help me with this one and I'll give you a big surprise." Her hand reached across John's thigh.

John was immediately uncomfortable. On the one hand, this woman was much drunker than he had initially surmised. She was attractive, and she was available. All he had to do was smile and act stupid for a short time, and she'd be his. Then his glance caught Mary's again, and he felt awkward and ill at ease, as though he'd be cheating on Mary if he were to leave with this woman. Why were these thoughts crossing his mind? Why did he really care about Mary? He'd just met her, for God's sake.

John glanced at Mary with guilt etched across his face. She looked at him briefly and returned her attention to Lisa.

John spoke with the woman in the beaver pants as Mary spoke to Lisa. Oddly enough, her name was Mary also. Is there nothing unique in this town? John thought.

The hands of Beaver-Skinned Mary, as John mentally dubbed her, started scrubbing his legs and massaging his arms as she told the long and rather boring story of her life. John smiled at the appropriate moments and acted concerned when she spoke of less attractive times. Her upper body was in a constant state of undulation as she attempted to brush John's arms with her breasts. She leaned close to his face and clung tightly to his leg, at times, for emphasis. At one point, she made sure that John noticed as she opened the top two buttons of her blouse to reveal more of her beautifully tanned, though slightly wrinkled, cleavage.

John had a nagging sense that this was a woman who had spent too much time in the sun and in other men's beds. She had been squeezed too many times by too many hands. Thankfully, she had taken John's mind off of the miserable atmosphere of Clayton, but, for a moment, he found it sad that her hair was not gray, that her clothes were not more age appropriate, that she didn't even attempt to be something other than a woman looking for a man in the basest sense. For all the time she must have spent trying to look young and beautiful, John saw only a wrung-out, old woman before him.

Finally, she could wait no longer. She leaned close to John and, with her warm, alcohol-laced breath, whispered. "Let's leave this place. Let's go to your place and be wild." Her tongue slid along the edge of her teeth as she emphasized the last word. Her eyes grew wider and glowed in anticipation. She grabbed his upper thigh, digging her fingers into his skin.

Desire was in her eyes, in her hands, and in her mouth. She drew her face closer to his. To John, it seemed as though she wanted to kiss him right there, in front of everyone. For a moment, he thought that it might not be bad to spend some time with someone who was doing everything she could to stop time and its process. At the very least, it would be another story to add to the sleepy stories about nothing he and his friends told at the bar. After all, he reasoned, he'd been with worse.

All of a sudden, John felt a gentle tapping on his left shoulder. It was the pale, beautiful hand of the other Mary. Her face was less gentle now, her manner more impatient, and her demeanor one of some consternation.

"Lisa just left, John. Isn't it time that we continue our talk?"

Beaver-Skinned Mary's face grew angry, its features contorted. "Who the heck is she? Who are you, pale face?" She looked like an old drunk now, disappointed that the man she was certain she had captured was going to fall out of her grasp.

John felt sheepish and defensive. "This is a friend... We met earlier. I promised I'd chat with her for a while."

"And so you jerked me around while you waited for her? What kind of guy are you, anyway?" Her voice was getting louder and sounding drunker. John was embarrassed and didn't know how to get out of the room without creating a bigger scene. He hated scenes.

"I didn't mean to jerk you around." He was beginning to feel ill. "We were just talking. I didn't mean..."

"You call what we were doing 'talking'? I'd hate to see what happens when you decide to flirt. Does anyone keep their clothes on?"

"I'm sorry, I don't know what to say…"

"Just get out of here. Take Ms. Polly Purebred home and leave me alone, you bastard."

Mary smiled as she locked her arm in John's. "Let's go, John. We can talk elsewhere. Please take 'Ms. Purebred' someplace civilized so we can speak." She kissed him lightly on the cheek as a final insult to Beaver-Skinned Mary.

Mary laughed as she and John reached the sidewalk outside the bar. "Ms. Purebred, indeed. Let's go somewhere to talk. Do you have any ideas? As I said before, I don't know the town very well."

John was beginning to overcome his feelings of discomfort and embarrassment at the scene in which he had just been involved. He looked at Mary. She was still smiling at him. "I have a room at the hotel not far from here."

Mary smiled at him again. "You move right along, don't you?"

John returned to his flustered state, stammering slightly as he spoke. "I didn't mean anything by it. We can just sit in the lobby or the parlor. It's just a nice, quiet place."

Mary's laughter cured John of his embarrassment and brought him back into her world again. The thought crossed his mind that he had already had one incredible night in one sleepy town—the best night he had had in some time. The rain had stopped, and he felt like the evening sun was shining on the streets of Clayton that night.

John paused for a moment before the large plate glass window which was the centerpiece of Mad Mike's. Inside the bar, he saw that Beaver-Skinned Mary had ordered another drink. Tucked tightly in her hand was a cocktail napkin stained with mascara. Tears still flowed slowly from the corner of each eye and ran quickly down the sides of her face. Along the way, they picked up stray oils from old makeup and dust from mascara that had been too generously applied earlier that evening. Her eyes were red and swollen. She looked down at the brown freckles on the backs of her hands and rubbed them hard. To John's eyes it appeared as if she were hoping they would disappear. John shook his head and returned his attention to Pale Mary.

She looked into John's eyes as they walked. "Were you really going to go home with her? Would you have taken advantage of that poor, old woman?"

John smiled slightly. "She wasn't that old. She had her own beauty about her. Besides, I am a man, you know."

"Being a man is not an excuse for brutish behavior. One can't attribute their own lack of a moral compass to their gender. It doesn't work that way."

John smiled again. His argument was weak and he knew it. As the couple approached the hotel, an odd feeling overtook John that he didn't have the courage to enunciate. He was hearing only his own footfalls again.

He was with another person, yet hearing only one set of footfalls. He thought that this was incredibly odd. His mind was racing. Did this mean that he had finally connected with the right person and they were walking as one, or did it mean that Pale Mary didn't really exist, that she couldn't exist in Clayton or anywhere else in the world? Not wanting Mary to think him odd, he did not tell her what was going through his mind.

Mary snuggled close to John as they walked. She smiled and leaned her head against his shoulder. His was a shoulder that she judged to be strong and very masculine. This man seemed kind and gentle. Perhaps he was a little bit "off the beam," as her grandmom would say. Still, there was strength and tenderness in his arms, frustration and cynicism in his face. The man was a mass of confused images. Mary wanted to know him better. She knew that the minute she caught him casting furtive glances at her in the bar.

John looked briefly at Mary's smiling face and into her beautiful blue eyes. This was a woman beyond him, a beauty that he did not deserve. How could something so wonderful happen to him in a town so lacking in so many other ways?

"Did you enjoy seeing Lisa again?"

The pale, cold blue of Mary's eyes met John's and found a place in his brain with which he was not comfortable. "She's become a bit strange over the years. We are very different now than we were—aren't you? Still, there is some basis in our being which we will always share because of the times we spent together when we were younger. Did you ever have a friend like that in your life?"

John was a bit taken aback by Mary's question. He had settled his gaze and his attention on the beauty of her face, the sheer softness of her hair. Her eyes were as steady and direct as the words she spoke. John had been absorbed into Mary's presence without totally listening to every word she said. "Um. Well, no. Well…wait yes. My childhood friend Bob and I were inseparable as children. As we grew older, we grew apart and became distant to each other. It was as if we never knew each other, but yet, on some basis we always will. Our childhood memories never really die."

Mary's eyes brightened at John's response, and she continued her thoughts without directly responding to John, though she thought her views were on point. "The world used to stretch out before us, but it's now behind us. We stand together and we stand separately. We stand alone and in a group that never dies. Who we were no longer exists. Who we are is up for discussion. Like you and your friend Bob, we once shared a profound moment in our lives, a moment of growth, a moment of maturity, a moment we can never lose because it is basic to our existence. So, while we will forever grow apart like two branches growing on one tree, we will always share the same root. We will always be friends, but our friendship will never grow because the point of overlap exists, but is buried deep in our past."

Mary's eyes glistened as she turned her full attention to John's face and playfully changed the subject. "And now you and I are marching across a hotel lobby in Clayton, Missouri, looking for your room. Do you remember where your room, or the elevator which might lead to your room, is located?"

John was in a state of date panic. He didn't know what to say. Finally, he just blurted out the thought running through his mind. "Lisa is a bit strange? Does that mean you are, too?"

Mary smiled. Her head tilted back, the sheath of hair flowing with her in a way that made her look particularly beautiful; her perfect white teeth were complemented by the deep red lipstick that surrounded them. Was it possible that she looked more beautiful than John had previously imagined? Certainly the lightness of her being filled the lobby with the crisp, clean feeling of a cataract in the midst of a country stream fed by melting snow. Mary's smile melted the snow and caused the troubles that walked with John on a daily basis to evaporate. For a moment, there was a feeling of lightness in his heart that he had not felt for years. For a moment, there was a purity in his life that he had forgotten long ago.

Mary looked into his eyes with her eyes glistening.

"You are a very funny man!"

"Funny, haha? Or, funny, strange?"

Mary twisted her head slightly and squinted her eyes as she looked into John's face. "You seem different. You are funny—humorous, and yet there seems to be a deep cynicism rooted in your being. It's a constant sadness, a desire unfulfilled."

"We are all wretched, after all." John responded without thinking.

Mary's eyes grew wide with genuine surprise. "Are we now? Are we really all wretched?" She stared at John coquettishly and asked, "Do you think I'm wretched?"

"Well, if you must know, yes. We are all truly wretched in God's eyes."

"God?" Mary was floored. "When did He enter into this discussion? You aren't some sort of weird religious type are you?"

"Well…no. But isn't perfection the concept we should all strive for? Isn't that the basis for all comparison? The being most typical cares about the temperature of his tea or the timeliness of his train. We have all given up on striving for perfection a long time ago. God is just a uniform standard of perfection for me. He doesn't have to be the being you studied in Sunday school."

John reached for the button to summon the elevator, but Mary grasped his hand before he could touch it. "I never went to Sunday school." With that, she pulled his body close to hers and kissed him with all the passion that was in her. John was overwhelmed and thrilled all at once. This type of thing never happened to him. After what seemed like five minutes, Mary's lips released his; she smiled and looked into his eyes.

"I didn't have to go to Sunday school," she said with an attitude that was almost defiant and yet tempered with a certain deep sensuality. "I was the daughter of the Sunday school teacher. Now let's go upstairs and you can teach this Sunday schoolgirl all about how wretched men make love."

● ● ●

The rain was still pouring down in Clayton, Missouri. John could hear it as it fell upon the faux patio and slapped against the shutters. He could still see the horrible art, the door to nowhere, the phone he had slammed down in his boss's ear a few short hours before. John could smell sex in the room. He could see every curve of Mary's supine body lying naked beside him in the grayish blue darkness. Her hair was fine and perfect; her breathing was lithe and gentle—if you didn't know it, you would swear that she was not breathing at all. Once in a while, her body would move slightly, and each curve would change its contour to create a different image of perfection. With the calming sound of rain in the background, he lay awake for hours studying each part of her body. Finally he fell asleep.

The next thing John knew, sunlight was streaming

into his room. He awoke with a start. His bed was empty. Mary was gone. In fifteen minutes, he was going to be late for the first meeting he had scheduled for that day. He shook his head to get his bearings. Where the hell was Mary? Was his money still here? He checked for his wallet and all was in place. Had Mary been a dream?

He found her note on the vanity. The handwriting was a beautiful script, perfectly formed and formatted. She would meet him for lunch at Ray's by Broadway and Main. If he didn't come, she'd understand that he didn't want to see her again. John ran to the shower to begin to get ready. He wanted to look perfect for Mary. There was a purpose to his life that he'd not felt for years. There was a feeling in his heart that he'd never felt before. There was a beautiful woman waiting to meet him for lunch, and he couldn't wait to see her. He was as happy as he'd ever been in his life.

John canceled his meeting and rushed to check out of the hotel. He left his bags with the concierge. His feet hit the streets of Clayton in a frenzy and with more energy than any foot had ever hit any path in sleepy old Clayton before. John ignored the fact that he heard only his own footfalls again. John ignored the fact that the town was too symmetrical and boring. John ignored the fact that his walk had quickened to a brisk trot in anticipation of meeting Mary again. People stared at this strange, panting man and he did not notice. As he approached Broadway and Main, he could see Ray's restaurant across the street. In the distance, he thought he saw Mary, her elegant stride and her beautiful black coat, and that fine blonde hair. In a town like this, beauty stands out like a beacon on a lonely jetty, he thought. John called her name and began to run when he suddenly felt a tightness in his chest, a pain running down the side of his arm. He fell flat on his face and was dead before he hit the sidewalk on the corner. Passersby stopped, police came, but no one knew this man or why he was in Clayton.

A red door with peeling paint opened and the town's richest drunk passed some money to the woman leaving the building. She stuffed the cash into her beaver skin pants and fussed with her shirt. The pants that were too tight had not been buttoned correctly, and the tail of her blouse hung over the waistband.

She scowled as she noticed the commotion on the street and went to see what had happened. The police were taking statements as she approached. "I know that guy," she volunteered. "He helped me with the crosswords at Mad Mike's last night. He left with a real bimbo, a working girl, you know? She probably wore him out." The police took down her inaccurate statement and her inaccurate description, and she left smiling. The rest of the crowd, hearing the story of a prostitute's involvement in this man's life, decided his death wasn't worth much either and, after a time, dispersed.

Of course, Mary had seen the commotion across the street. It wasn't her way to rubberneck in life. That was what others did, not she. Besides, she didn't want to miss John if he came into the restaurant while she was outside. After an hour of waiting, she decided he wasn't coming. She was surprised. She thought they had hit it off well. She shrugged her shoulders and headed to the airport. She decided that all he had really wanted was quick sex; it made her sad, but it didn't surprise her. After all, he had made that "I am a man" comment.

9/11/2001
The Tear That
Refused to Fall

Chloe sat at the bus stop with her cello. The cello was in its solid white case, and drops of water began to slide off its edges as the morning mist morphed into a light rain. There was a tear at the corner of Chloe's eye that simply refused to fall. She sat staring across the street, finding the spaces between old oak trees that stood before the 19th-century Victorian homes with wraparound porches. The house paint was peeling in the rain. The roots of the trees on her side of the street were pushing up the sidewalk. The cement's upheaval had caused three people to trip since Chloe first arrived and took her seat across from the white oaks and white houses. Chloe stared straight ahead with an absentminded melancholy etched onto her face. The last few days had seemed like an eternity. Her life had changed so completely that she couldn't remember the way things were a week ago. She did not know Abu. Abu did not know her.

There were trees on this street that she could not name. Cars that Chloe didn't really notice moved by her in uneven clumps. Molded steel and monoxide gas could not penetrate the concentrated apathy that had overtaken her. Life had long since lost its excitement. She knew that people rarely agreed with her view of things. She had learned that no one really cared. There was no one left on this planet for Chloe. She released an audible sigh and allowed herself a peek at the watch on her wrist.

Chloe smiled thinly as she realized that there was no watch. She had not worn one for years; why care about what time it was now? She looked down the street and wondered when the bus would arrive. Chloe tapped the cello case beside her and dabbed at the tear that lurked at the corner of her eye. She allowed herself a sniffle as her fingers found her black curly hair and twisted the curls tighter than they had been.

Stan was dead, of course, as were so many others. Chloe didn't think that she had ever really loved him, though she had told him that she did so many times. He didn't really love her either, and she knew it. She shook her head quickly from side to side, resembling a large chocolate Lab on the hunt, as bits of water sprayed in all directions from her perfectly curly hair. Mercifully, her bright green eyes were covered for a moment by her closed lids, and Chloe renewed her vow to ignore all things negative.

So many people traveled with Chloe in the canyons of her mind. So many personalities still meant something to her, and yet they meant nothing at all. Were she to renew these old acquaintances, she thought that she would be bored or disappointed by all. Worse, she could fall in love again and regret the millions of seconds she would have missed without the mystery lover's magnificent company. But about whom was she thinking? Was she ever in love? Did she ever know happiness, that transitory moment one realizes between exquisite eternities of despair? Laughter? She'd experienced laughter often, but couldn't recount one reason to laugh today.

She closed her eyes and shook her head again. She'd forgotten about her pledge to ignore all things negative.

A very fat woman with a shirt too tight ambled by Chloe and her cello and sat at the other end of the bench. Chloe looked at the woman briefly and without any interest. She then turned back to the cars that passed before her on a street that was becoming very wet.

The woman at the other end of the bench rubbed her eyes and nose in one motion. Her eyes were sunk in large craters of fat as she squinted down the street. Chloe felt an internal smile beginning to develop as she tried to imagine what the woman could possibly be looking for as she looked down the street. The woman turned her attention to Chloe and spoke.

"Bus coming soon?"

The woman swallowed her words as she spoke, but Chloe got the gist of her question.

Opening her eyes wide and blinking three times,

Chloe pointed to her mouth, pretending she couldn't speak. She shook her head no and made some guttural noises for added effect.

The woman was horrified. She did not know what to do. After a moment, she nodded to Chloe and smiled, then looked over her right shoulder to see if there was someone else who might rescue her from the uncomfortable situation.

When she realized that the two of them were alone and there would be no help forthcoming, she smiled at Chloe again, shrugged her shoulders, and gazed across the street.

Success, thought Chloe, beaming from within. Her little ruse had worked with the old plump one, and now she'd be left alone. The twinkle in her eye was genuine. Her happiness was real, though short-lived. Stan was dead. Now what was she going to do?

Then she remembered. Lisa was coming to her house, and she needed to clean up. It had seemed so long since Chloe had last seen Lisa, her dear and trusted friend. Lisa was a lovely person. She cared about Chloe, and Chloe knew that her concern was sincere.

Chloe looked down the street one more time. Then she looked at the woman seated beside her again and shook her shoulders. She picked up her wet cello case and began to walk away. The woman swallowed hard and called after her.

"Moving on, huh? Giving up on the bus?"

For a moment, Chloe forgot all about her ruse of pretending that she could not speak. For a moment, there was clarity in the situation that shook Chloe in a way that she had not often experienced. For a moment, Chloe wanted to make the move that would unite her thoughts and speech, to move her eyes from that place where she watched herself speak to a point where her eyes, speech, and presence would exist together at a normal, human boundary. Chloe decided to say what she thought to the stranger who was waiting for the bus. .

"I have moved on. The world has moved on. Don't you see that?"

The woman looked as if she had just tasted some very bad fish. She was confused and put off by the odd response of the odd woman who carried the odd-shaped box which was now drenched with water. Not knowing what to say, she just shook her head and looked for an approaching bus that couldn't get there fast enough for her.

As Chloe walked home, the rain fell harder and her curls formed a matted outline that framed her face. The extreme paleness of her countenance was only heightened by the absence of sun and the presence of rain. She wore a black cotton shirt over her black jeans, which flopped over her black, high-topped shoes. She was vaguely attractive, with a natural beauty that had been somewhat creased by the passage of time. The intense color present in her eyes was the key to understanding her existence. There was a time when those eyes would twinkle and glow at a joke well told or a bit of juicy gossip; now there was a certain feeling of intense vacancy to her eyes, like the lifeless glare of a shark. They provided neither insight into the soul of her being nor proof that a soul actually existed. When one stared into Chloe's eyes, one could sense an unimpeachable feeling of uncertainty surrounded by a steely passivity that caused one to question the emotional stability of the person standing before you.

Chloe was now soaked to the bone. Umbrellas were in full bloom on both sides of the sidewalk. She felt like the only one on the street who lacked protection against the elements. She thought about lifting the cello case over her head, but decided that that would not be practical.

Chloe looked at every umbrella-protected face as they passed her in the rain, but few returned her stare. "Are they ashamed to be protected when I am not?" thought Chloe. "Why should today be different than any other day?"

Chloe shook her head and shed more droplets as she walked. The rain was falling hard; rivulets of water ran around the contours of her eyebrows and united with the tear at the corner of her eye. Finally, Chloe felt comfortable wiping moisture away from her eyes. She sniffled slightly as she wiped away the rivulets and thought for a moment about how bad she felt.

One never knows when a "life moment" will occur, thought Chloe. Most moments are products of extensive deconstruction or people trying to make something out of meaningless history. In her case, there was no doubting she had experienced her "life moment," but all anyone could say was that she must "move on." This was the most important event in her life, and everyone wanted her to forget it. Why?

It was time for Chloe to go home and clean her apartment. Lisa was coming over; the place should be clean. A bus roared by as Chloe slowly turned up the walkway that led to her apartment door.

The dead leaves of autumn lined her path as she approached the door. Large, wet maple and oak leaves that had blown from nearby trees matted together and formed odd patterns on Chloe's lawn. There were Dusty Millers on either side of the walk near her newly painted red door. They looked limp and lifeless as they prepared for winter's cold and death. Chloe paused for a moment to consider them before she went in.

As she entered her immaculate apartment, she left her white, wet cello case standing against the wall. She reached for a dish towel to dry her hair. She removed her wet shoes and left them by the door. Next Chloe took off her socks, pants, and wet cotton shirt and piled them up on a towel she had left by the door.

For a moment, Chloe stood naked in the kitchenette

by the entrance to her apartment. She had shed all that had touched the world outside and paused for a moment to consider her body. In an absentminded way, Chloe stroked different curves on her body and found them soft and pretty. She had not considered herself as a woman in some time. For a moment, she felt connected to that excited young girl who had fallen for Stan so long ago.

Shaking her head again, she ran upstairs to change. She found her favorite black wool sweater and black jeans. As she pulled her clothes on, she looked in the mirror and felt sexy; it was so odd, a thought so out of place for her.

She ran back downstairs and gathered the laundry by the door. She didn't want her clothes to puddle there, so she rushed to the washer and dumped them in. A little soap was all they would need to be clean.

As the washer began its cycle, Chloe slammed her head. "Forgot the towel." She ran to the door, grabbed the towel, and tossed it into the washer.

"There," she said to no one in particular. "Much better."

Chloe's eyes surveyed her spotless apartment as she looked for something to clean. Her television set was caked with dust. It stood out as a part of her place that needed attention. She refused to touch it. She did not know Abu and Abu did not know her.

She stood before the television set momentarily puzzled, wondering what she should do next. Instinctively, her eyes stared directly at the telephone lying in wait in its cradle. The evil instruments of mankind sat before her, taunting her, letting her know that they would never go away. A momentary trembling overtook her body and spirit. Chloe felt nauseated as she looked at the ivory-colored demon before her; she prayed that it would not ring. Again, she shook her head and regrouped. "No negativity!" she reemphasized to herself.

She needed to move from that spot in the room, but the spot held her feet to the floor. The spot held her heart. The spot held her soul. The spot held her life until she could find a way to move further down the line again.

"Cheese!" she thought, "I need cheese and crackers for my guest." Chloe ran to her well-organized refrigerator, took out a block of cheese, and began to cut it into very thin slices.

Next, she raced to the cupboard, removed the crackers, and arranged them in a perfectly straight row on a plate. She repackaged the remaining crackers and returned them to their space in the cupboard.

The ringing of her front doorbell startled Chloe. She moved quickly to answer the door.

Lisa stood there, dripping and smiling, in a pretty green wool hat whose brim protected her bright green eyes from the rain. Lisa's eyes were radiant and alive. They sparkled with a freshness reserved for those much younger than she. Her skin was without blemish, and her red hair could not be contained within the boundaries of her freshly soaked hat. Lisa wore a deep red coat, blue jeans, and running shoes (though Chloe was relatively sure that Lisa never ran anywhere). Her perfectly white smile was her most attractive quality. It reflected her enduring good cheer and an enthusiasm rarely shown in other people Chloe had met.

Standing beside Lisa, besotted and shifting his weight from one foot to the other, was a good-looking man framed in wet gray wool without a cap. His face was drawn, tight, and tense, as though expressing his desire to be anywhere but on Chloe's porch at this wet time.

"Hi, Chloe!" Lisa had drawn out the first syllable of her greeting a few extra beats to express her utter glee at being in the company of her friend. She reached out to hug Chloe around the neck. "How are you doing, my love? I've missed you! What have you been up to?"

Chloe's eyes began to tear slightly at the sight of Lisa. "I'm fine," she said, as she gave Lisa two light taps on the back. "But where are my manners? Come in, come in. Is he with you?"

Lisa smiled at Chloe's sarcasm and slapped her shoulder. "Yes, he's with me. Come in, Mark. Chloe…Mark, Mark…Chloe," she said, gesturing from one to the other.

Mark looked even more uncomfortable in the phosphorescent glow of Chloe's apartment. "Hi Chloe, I have been looking forward to meeting you," he said without conviction.

Putting on her British accent, Chloe said, "Charmed, I'm sure." She extended her right hand to Mark. Then a bell went off in her head. "Not enough cheese cut. We'll need more. Come to the kitchen, you two."

Chloe took out the cheese and feverishly cut more slices. Lisa smiled at her friend while Mark eyed the incredible order of Chloe's apartment. Cheese cut, crackers served, Chloe opened one of the two bottles of wine that Lisa had brought.

Lisa and Chloe began to talk, and Mark tried to contribute where he could. The more wine he drank, the more his attention began to waver, and he became increasingly fascinated by the eerie cleanliness of Chloe's apartment. Mark was trying to understand the relationship between Chloe and Lisa. Without any prior introduction to Chloe, he wanted to learn what he could by listening to the women speak and watching them interact with each other. He found it strange that Lisa always seemed to need to touch a part of Chloe's body as they spoke. They held hands. Lisa gently touched Chloe's shoulder or wrist as she stared intently into Chloe's eyes. It was as if Lisa was trying to tether Chloe to the ground or keep her from spinning into space with her contact. Occasionally, Lisa would smile at Mark as she spoke to Chloe or slip him a surreptitious look, in silent appreciation of his patience.

Still, Mark had little else to do than drink, so drink he did. Soon he had opened up the second bottle of wine and decided that, with or without the help of the others, he was going to finish it.

The women were speaking about a book they had read when Mark realized he needed to find the bathroom. He asked Chloe to direct him. The directions she gave seemed a bit involved, but he was a wee bit drunk and he followed her directions to the letter. On the way back, Mark decided to explore Chloe's apartment.

He was absolutely stupefied by the immaculate apartment. It was antiseptically clean, like a hospital. He saw order breaking out everywhere he looked. He turned a corner and found himself in the living room, at the center of which was a large television.

For a moment, Mark thought that he had finally found his savior. He could watch television, while Lisa and Chloe spoke all night about whatever they wished. But what dust! What was the dust all about? It was as if all the dust that could have ever accumulated in this apartment were deposited on the television. He reached out his hand to wipe off the screen. The thickness of the dust was repulsive to him. He decided that he'd turn on the set first and ask for the dust rag later. He looked for the power switch and turned on the television.

The static electricity caused by the accumulated

dust and the touch of a human hand caused the television to crackle as it powered on. The sound of the crackle was loud enough to be heard throughout Chloe's small apartment.

Chloe froze. For a moment, shock and despair battled for control of her facial features. Her eyes grew wide and began to tear immediately. For a split second, she stared at Lisa in stunned silence. Then, she started to shriek, "Nooo! Not the TV." She ran to Mark, ripped the remote from his nervously fumbling hands, and hurled it against the wall. "Not TV. No TV." Chloe was wailing as she ran to her bedroom. Lisa tried to run after her, but Chloe begged her to leave.

Lisa returned from Chloe's hallway with fire in her eyes as she gathered Mark and their belongings. "You," she said, addressing Mark in a tone that he'd never heard before. "Put this stuff on." She flung his coat at him. "We are leaving this apartment, NOW!" The emphasis she had placed on the last word of the sentence told Mark that something incredibly serious had just taken place, though he had no clue as to what it was.

They left Chloe's apartment in a whirlwind of anger and despair.

Chloe looked at the picture of Stan in the crystal frame that stood on her bedside table. She saw him again. She had not seen him in so, so long. Then Chloe looked at the crystal that surrounded him. The cold perfection of crystal frightened her—how could it really exist? The imperfection that was Stan was reflected in that image. It reminded her of so many things. Chloe put her head on the pillow and cried herself to sleep.

Lisa was livid; Mark was drunk and confused. They flew down the pathway, Lisa's fingers wrapped tightly around Mark's arm, practically pulling him along the sidewalk. Her face was flushed. Mark was trying to figure out what was wrong and what he should say. He was pretty convinced that no matter what he did at that moment, Lisa was not going to appreciate it. Still, he had to try. At least he might be able to slow their ridiculous pace.

"I don't know what I did, Lisa, but I'm sorry."

Lisa's hair was flying as she moved. The fire in her eyes and in her manner could not be quenched by the tears that poured down her cheeks.

"One question." She stopped walking and stood nose to nose with Mark on the sidewalk. "Do you ever listen to a word I say?"

The alcohol in Mark's veins had an easy, flip reply prepared, but the look on Lisa's face prevented him from being anything but serious.

"Of course I do."

"Do you remember the story I told you about my friend from Boston? The woman I was speaking to on the phone on 9/11?"

"You told me about a few different women you spoke

to that day, and others that you couldn't contact. Which one are you talking about?"

"Idiot!" Lisa pushed Mark backwards as she slammed his shoulders. "Chloe was the one I was speaking to as we watched replay after replay of the plane crashing into the tower. Chloe was the one who was so sad for all the victims because her husband often did business there. Chloe was the one who told me that she felt so privileged because Stan was safe on a plane headed for California as we watched in horror. That is, until she realized that she was watching a replay of her husband's death, over and over, as his plane flew into the tower."

The alcohol left Mark's system and an awful reality replaced it. "She collapsed on the phone," Lisa continued. "I had to call the Boston police to get her out of her house. She's never really moved on from that day." Lisa was crying uncontrollably now, and Mark moved to hug her.

"I told you not to touch her television. I asked you to stay within the boundaries of Chloe's conversation. How could you forget? How could you turn on that blasted TV?"

"I was drunk. I didn't make the connection," Mark said lamely. "I'm sorry. I'm really, really sorry."

Lisa looked at Mark. "I know. Please take me home." Lisa knew the relationship was over.

After Lisa arrived home, she sat and thought about

Chloe for a while. She knew she had to call her. She just didn't know what to say. Chloe answered on the second ring, her voice sleepy.

"I didn't mean to wake you, Chloe. I just want to apologize."

"It's okay, Lisa, it isn't your fault. I've got to control myself better."

"It was just such a stupid screwup. Mark wasn't thinking."

Chloe was angered by that comment, but she did not communicate her anger to Lisa.

"I understand. I have to get by it. Every day, I think that I am getting better. Every day, I think that I am moving on. Yesterday, I saw a huge field of brown cornstalks twisted, broken, falling on top of each other. The field was a sad testimony to destruction. It was filled with broken, dead bodies. It was so sad. It has been a real struggle for me, you know. There was so much said that should have been unsaid, so much unsaid that should have been said. Our relationship had deteriorated and I still mourn. I should have been better. Why wasn't I more to him?"

"You've got to stop beating yourself up," Lisa said. "You were what you could be to Stan. You need to move on now, Chloe."

Chloe's body stiffened at the other end of the phone in an almost robotic reaction to Lisa's last comment. "You're right, Lisa. I need to move on. I've got to go now.

I'm still a bit upset. Can I call you another time?"

"Sure," Lisa said. "But promise you will call me, okay?"

"Promise." Chloe tried to brush away the tear at the corner of her eye.

Lisa hung up, satisfied that she had made peace with her friend. Worried that Chloe was still so raw in her emotions, hoping that their friendship could move on, Lisa picked up her purse and went to the mall. She had had a rough day, and she needed to get lost in a crowd again.

Chloe heard Lisa hang up and threw the receiver at the mirror that stood at the foot of her bed. The mirror cracked in so many directions, but it did not break. Chloe took off all of her clothes and looked at herself in the cracked mirror. "I must move on." Chloe pulled back the covers on her bed and lay naked on the sheets. She fell asleep.

The next day, Chloe rose and looked at the cracked mirror before her, puzzled. She shook her head slightly and moved towards her bathroom to take a shower and get dressed. Her cello case stood by the door as it always did. Today, she was going to the train station. She picked up her cello and went towards the door. She saw the wine bottles, the wine glasses, the crackers and thinly sliced cheese still sitting in the kitchen. It was not a bad dream. It had really happened to her. She did not know Abu and Abu did not know her.

Visto's Church
An Apologue

The sun reflected from the bright white shingles of the small but well-kept church that sat atop the otherwise desolate hill. A black limousine pulled up in front of the church, and a small, black-haired man in a black suit opened the door and went in.

The church was dim on one side; the windows were open; the chirping of birds was heard and yet suspended. The solemn silence of this house seemed to consume any noise that dared venture within. The dark-suited visitor eyed the wooden pews and the font of holy water which stood before him. Slowly and solemnly, he dipped his hand into the water, genuflected, and began to walk towards the altar. Was it a waffling of purpose or the impenetrable silence of this house that made the visitor hesitate as he walked?

The stained glass windows showed patterns on the floor that changed with every wind that blew the tree branches outside. On one wall he spied the Stations of the Cross; the sight of them made him shudder slightly.

The confessionals behind him then captured the visitor's glance; he paused for a moment before the statue of Saint Joseph and bowed his head as if he were in prayer. Slowly, he knelt.

Tears streaked down the side of his face as he rose from his prayer and stuck a bill in the poor box. He walked to the center of the altar and stared for a moment at the body of Christ on a crucifix above the altar. Wiping away the tears, he genuflected again. Spying the door that led to the pastor's room, he went in. The hall was dimly lit by the ceiling lights. Finally the door was before him. The nameplate read: Pastor Visto. Slowly, the visitor began to knock.

"What? Who's there? Is that you, Stanley? Sorry, I could raise no money for you this week. Well, get in here man; I can't even hear you."

The visitor placed his hand on the bronze, oval-shaped doorknob and twisted it to the left. The door would not open. He twisted the knob to the right and opened the door.

"As I said, there's no money. Your fellow parishioners are as poor as you and I. But what can we do? Just continue to do what we can, right? We'll see our way through, right?"

The dark visitor had entered the room in the middle of the pastor's speech. The darkness in the room swallowed up all light that tried to penetrate it. Three slats of light fell upon an open Bible, which sat on a large mahogany desk. Two hands could be seen in the indistinct gloom. A body must have belonged to those hands, but the visitor could not see it. The room was a dark black box in a dull gray grid. It smelled manila and off white, yellow and dusty.

Throughout the pastor's speech, the visitor focused his eyes upon the bony, pale hands.

"Right, Stanley, right? What's wrong with you today? Have you no tongue?"

At last the dark man spoke. "I am not Stanley. My name is Roger. I have come to confess my sins, Father. May I sit down?"

The demeanor of the old priest changed suddenly.

"I've never met you before, Roger. I don't recognize your voice. Are you a new member of our parish? I'd be pleased to welcome another member to our parish." The old priest was visibly nervous as his fingers stroked the Bible on the desk. "Why have you come to see me today?"

The visitor slowly straightened his tie. "I've already told you, my Father, I want to confess my sins. Will you not hear my confession?"

The old withered hands moved away from the light on the Bible. A slight fumbling could be heard in the darkness. Perhaps the old priest was putting on the proper vestments for the sacrament. "Very slowly now, sir, please tell me your sins."

Once again, the visitor fidgeted with his tie. "Father,

I am a professional criminal. My business has been the breaking of God's commandments. I killed my mother and father for my own advancement. I have had many adulterous affairs. I have stolen and I have lied. It seems that I have broken every law of God and man."

The priest's shaking hands returned to his Bible, where he began stroking the pages before him. Then, he clenched his fists.

"I know of no penance which could redeem you in God's eyes. I cannot see you; I do not know how old you are, but if you began to serve the Lord today, he would have a right to refuse you entrance into heaven."

The dark man stared at the floor for a moment and seemed to be reciting something to himself before he spoke. "But what of the prayer of the Lord? Does it not say, 'Forgive us our trespasses as we forgive those who trespass against us'?"

The old priest's hands struck the Bible before him as he spoke. He was becoming frustrated and angry.

"How can I dole out a proper penance? Perhaps you should trust your luck to the mercy of God. I would appreciate it if you left my chamber immediately. The quickest exit is downstairs and to the left."

"I'd suggest that you do not cross the altar of the Lord lest he dole out his sentence for your blasphemous conduct before your appointed time. I am a poor priest who sits in this impenetrable gloom all day, but I can see that evil has consumed you and spat you out before me. Your penance is denied. Leave the house of the Lord." The priest had risen and begun to bellow as he finished his speech.

The dark visitor rose from his chair and leaned over the desk before the priest. His eyes glowed, his mouth quivered, and his skin breathed hate. Slowly, a more resolute look appeared on his face. Once more, he straightened his tie and sat down.

"I must begin my purgatory on Earth, holy Father. I could never endure the eternity of hell, alone and suffering for my earthly transgressions. Let the mercy of the church save my lost soul. I want to redeem myself. Please help me, Father."

The old priest sat down and sighed. "What should I do? Make you say a million Hail Marys? A thousand Our Fathers? One hundred Apostle's' Creeds? Cloister you away in an African mission? How should I save your soul? I feel that it is my duty to try to save you, but I fear that you cannot be saved."

"Most Holy Father," said the dark man, "I have a modest proposal. To pray alone is not enough. I would like to help my church in a more constructive way. Perhaps I could help the poor souls of your parish. I am very wealthy, my Father, and I'd like to put my wealth to good use."

The old priest could not reconcile himself to the

bargain proposed by the dark man. "Preposterous. You cannot use ill-gotten profits to serve the Lord. I will not have you serving your penance by corrupting the good people of this poor parish. Money may have bought all that you have desired before, but it will not buy the mercy of the Lord. It's just not that easy."

"I do not intend to buy the mercy of the Lord, Holy Father, I only wish to contribute to your parish in addition to my penance. Is it wrong to repent? Jesus forgave Judas, didn't he? I'll serve all penance and help build up the economic status of your parish. Will you let me do that, Father?"

"I do not deny that we could use the money, but I don't like it. The money is dirty with the sins of your past."

"Then let the future absolve my money from all its past sins and injustices. Please, Father, I really want to do this."

The old priest saw the compromise as a means to provide help to his parishioners, who all needed so much. "All right, my son, you shall have your way. We'll make this parish thrive through your contributions. Your penance is to live here and study the Bible with me until one of us dies. Do you agree to do this?"

"Yes, Father."

"Then move into the room next to mine. We shall tell the parishioners that you are my assistant. We shall not tell them that you are contributing any money to our organization. This compromise is a solution that shall be a secret that we shall share. I don't want my people to believe that there is an alternate path to salvation. Yours is a special case. You must maintain this vow of secrecy."

"Yes, Father."

• • •

Within a few years, the old priest's small parish was the richest in the state. The people seemed to become more devout as the quarters filled their coffers. Instead of collections at Sunday Mass, there was the dispensing of welfare checks. The dark visitor seemed to be a new man; each day his face grew brighter and his attitude cheerier.

One day, the visitor convinced the old priest to consult an oculist. The oculist said that the old man's blindness could be cured and began treatments.

The priest's vision came back in stages. At times he thought that he could see a human form. He would call to the visitor: "Matthew... James... John... Paul..." Each time the visitor would correct him.

"Sorry sir, I'm not he. It's Roger."

It was a beautifully bright summer Sunday when the old priest returned from his final treatment in New York. The entire parish waited outside after the Mass, which, for the first time, had been led by the dark visitor. They were eager to welcome their pastor home. Large, expensive cars now owned by the parishioners surrounded the church.

Hand-carved oak doors with golden knockers and brass knobs stood closed. The church had been insulated by the most expensive aluminum siding. Large marble statues of Saint Joseph and Michael the Archangel stood on either side of the marble staircase, which led to the doors. A marble statue of the Virgin Mary stood beneath a large tree. The garage which housed the old priest's limousines stood to the left of the church. The parking lot and driveways had just been re-pitched. The hill was a study in cluttered blacks and grays. The steeple of the church was also new. It was a solid gold cross that was about five feet tall.

Finally, someone in the crowd saw the priest's approaching limousine. The crowd cheered as the door opened. One of the priest's private nurses got out before him. Roger took his place before the doors of the church on the marble steps he had built, beside the statues that he had paid for, yet out of view of the golden cross he had bought for the old priest.

The old priest stepped out of the limo to the jubilant cries of the people. His private doctor followed him out of the car and held up his hand for silence.

"I decided to wait until we got here before I removed the patches from Pastor Visto's eyes. I feel that a man who is so dedicated to the good of his parish should see that parish first, and see the great things that he has given us all through the work of his own two hands."

Slowly and carefully, the doctor unraveled the bandages. When at last the priest's eyes were visible, he stood blinking in the sunlight. He rubbed his eyes and squinted at his church.

Slowly his vision seemed to come into focus. Was it the wonderment and great joy of first sight that put the astonished look on the pastor's face as he stared at the steps of his church? The crowd was silent; it could not understand what he had perceived.

Enlightenment, anger, fear, and anguish battled for control of his newly found sight as he blindly fumbled for his cross.

"Roger," he said. "It's you, Roger." A great gust of wind blew from some unseen valley. The great cross which Roger had bought for the old priest fell from the roof and divided the pastor in two.

The people of the parish screamed, united in horror. They ran to their cars and fled. Roger stood for a moment and looked at the old priest's remains. He smiled grimly.

"Compromise is the language of the devil, padre. Don't ever forget that." He bent over the body and smiled broadly.

"My work is done here." Roger went to his limousine and drove down the hill and to the left.

• • •

Today, the church still stands, though the statues have fallen, the doors are rotten, and leaves cover the marble stairs. No one ventures near the hill. It's said that the devil himself has taken over the church and the old man's bones lie there unburied and visible for those who wish to see.

Cinderella Has Cellulite

Jim sat on the black, high-backed seat with the olive green cushion, just as he'd always wanted to do. His eyes were bloodshot, though he didn't know it, and his eye sockets seemed somewhat sunken into his skull. Jim grasped the beer before him and took a deep draught. For a moment his eyelids were half closed, and then a tiny speck of light could be seen in a small portion of his pupil by those who cared to notice. Some would say that his eyes were twinkling; he would say that they were ablaze with the fire that still lingered in his soul. He smiled at his vision of himself and thought for a moment.

"Well, my friend, are you calling or folding?" She was on him again. He could not see her eyes, shaded as they were by the hat brim she had pulled down low upon her forehead. He had not seen her eyes all night, and it annoyed him. That was the only thing about her that annoyed him.

She wore square-toed Frye boots, of course, which were mostly hidden by the tight blue jeans that looked so perfect as they formed a thirty-degree angle from the crook of her boot to the top of her heel. Her pants were faded and slightly frayed; she looked gorgeous in them. She wore a bright white shirt with three buttons opened at the top and a brown suede vest over that. Her hair was long and brown; it hung over her shoulders with curls at the base that endeavored to touch and frame her face.

None of her hair touched her chest; to Jim there was something breathtakingly beautiful about that. She had the chest of a youthful beauty. There was not a mark upon it, and it glistened in the smoky haze and dim light that filled the room. If only he could see her eyes, her eyelashes, her brow! Then Jim's night would be complete. He was certain that her face was perfect, and yet, he'd seen nothing more than the tip of her nose, her chin, and her very loud mouth. The rest all lurked in the shadow.

"Calling or folding?" She repeated the words with more emphasis this time. She reached for a small, thin cigar and tossed it into her mouth like it was a cigarette. She grabbed a lighter and lit the cigar. She inhaled very slowly and blew the smoke into Jim's face. "Calling or folding?"

Jim called the bet. "Four Kings!" She laughed, rubbing her hands together. Jim had three Jacks. She laughed louder as she reached out, surrounded the pot with her arms, and brought it to her side of the table. She had won again. She reached out to Jim and touched his arm. She told him that he was her best friend at the poker table.

A feeling ran through Jim's body that he had never felt before. He looked down at the table so that his eyes would not betray his soul to the others. His body was trembling; his vision grew fuzzy for a moment. He could not understand how the touch of an arm could generate such feelings.

"Pear and pair; two, to, and too. They're all homonyms!" Maxi and Deidre were drunk again. Maxi had a thing for homonyms whenever she got drunk.

"Bear and bare; nice and ice." When Maxi was really drunk, she'd try to construct homonyms for words that had none. To those new to the party, Maxi would define a homonym at three thousand decibels—"words that sound the same but mean something different and are spelled differently—that's a homonym!" This was a sentence that was always punctuated by a drink and some knowing laughter by Maxi and Deidre (if she was there). Why homonyms? No one knew. One night, Maxi and Deidre had tried onomatopoeia without success. Only homonyms worked for them.

Maxi never wore nail polish, and she had long red hair that she often stuffed around her ears. Her blue jeans had thin white lines running through them to make them look faded. Her thighs were a little fat, as was her middle. She could not stand with her legs together and show the "three diamonds of perfection"; her legs were too fat for that!

Maxi had brought photos to show the group that night. Her old blue Ford had finally passed the 100,000-mile mark on her odometer, and she had taken pictures. Being Maxi, she had photographed not the car, but the odometer. The first picture showed 99999[8]. The "8" was in the white box to show it was a decimal. The next picture was 99999[9] with the "9" in the white box. The following picture was special: 00000[0]. The old Ford had made it to "Flipsville," as Maxi called it. The next picture was 00000[1], proving that the old Ford was on its way to another 100,000 miles. Who, but Maxi, would drive their car for four-tenths of a mile, stopping every tenth to record an event that was, at least for some, rather insignificant? But Maxi was proud of the achievement! After all the things that car had had to go through to reach 100,000 miles, Maxi felt it deserved honor and celebration.

From across the room, another inebriated voice joined the din. "Hey, Kennedy. I know you're a Kennedy. Let me see your license, Kennedy."

Jim drank some more beer.

Night after night, this guy refused to give up on his drunken assumption that Jim was somehow related to the Kennedys. Jim rolled his eyes and tossed his license at the drunken fellow's face—again informing him that he was not a Kennedy.

She poured Jim a shot of Cuervo and tilted her head back slightly as she spoke. "Are you going to play cards or run the country?" She smiled, and Jim could see perfectly white teeth between what he perceived to be perfectly red lips. For a fleeting moment, he thought that he saw her eyes and eyebrows, but before he could be sure, her head was down again, staring at a smoky glass half-filled with Cuervo Gold, shuffling cards, and smoking a cigar.

"Ante up, big boy." She attempted to playfully swat the back of his head. Jim played his ante, shot some tequila, and tried to sneak a look at her one more time.

Jim's eyes always focused on her chest; the light for the table seemed to focus on her chest, too, even though it was designed to focus on the table and the cards. Her chin was just inside the shadow. She had a small brown freckle or two, but beyond that, her chest seemed to glisten. Jim did not want to be caught staring, so he only cast a lingering glance or two that way. My God, she was beautiful.

A perfect smoke ring seemed to glide out of the darkness from her side of the table. It hovered over the chips for a second, dissipated, and then disappeared.

"Show me your real license, Kennedy. This is obviously the fake one they give you to fool people like me." A driver's license landed in the center of the table from points unknown. Jim rolled his eyes and put it in his pocket. Was there a homonym for "drunken dope"?

Jim drank some more beer.

"Lay and lei, like in Hawaii you know? Pour, poor, pore. Like... Pour me a beer, Jim. It is good for a poor drunk like me; soon beer sweat will come out of my pores. Homonyms—words that sound the same but are spelled differently." Maxi had progressed to that annoying stage she went through right before leaving the party or passing out on the floor. Jim shook his head and chuckled. She had an infectious laugh. She had so much life and spirit within her.

The music was getting louder as Jim drank some more beer. The cacophony reminded him that he didn't always love the music he heard when he played cards in Skeneatles. Someone was always too inebriated to select the perfect tune every time. It was getting late and Jim knew it. He would have to go home soon.

A shot glass was never far from her left hand; a bottle of Cuervo was never far from her right. She slammed the shot glass down upon the table to rouse those that needed it from the wonderful haze that had captured their faces and their minds. The lazy happiness in the room was being shared by all. Maxi had passed out on the couch, and others were nodding off amidst the stench of too much alcohol and too many cigarettes. The poker game had come round to the final hand, and she wanted Jim to have another shot of tequila before the night was over.

The other players at the table jumped slightly when she slammed the shot glass, but then returned to their sleepy postures, their heads propped up by their hands. Half-filled glasses of beer sat at various points on the table like numbers on a clock face.

Her chest still looked perfect in the hazy light of the poker table. Her hat was still pulled down over her eyes, and most of the chips were on her side of the table. All that, and a great poker player, too! Jim chuckled to himself. As he reached for the shot before him, she held her hand up; she was silently asking him to pause. With the shot in her right hand, she entwined her arm with his. They were going to do this last shot and finally gaze into each other's eyes. With her left hand, she took off her hat and shook her hair free. Wisps of smoke were blown away from the table as her face came out of the darkness to look into Jim's eyes.

"To my best friend at the poker table." She smiled a sweet and perfect smile. Her bright eyes glistened as she widened and then squinted them to adjust and focus in the light. Jim would always remember the piercing blue beauty of her eyes as she looked at him and smiled. He hesitated for a moment, and then they both drank their shots simultaneously, wordlessly staring at each other, inches apart, in the blue incandescent haze of the moment.

They finished their shots and slammed their glasses on the table. She smiled again and grasped Jim's hand in what seemed to be a profound mixture of friendship, estrangement, and love. The clasp lasted a few seconds longer than it should have.

They both blew out a sigh and let go. Jim had to go

and he knew it. Her friends were ready to leave. It was daybreak, and he stood at the door and waved to her as she left. She paused for a moment before she got into the car. Once again, her hat came off. Once again, her hair shook in the damp, foggy air of morning. She held out her arm and waved good-bye, "We'll see you soon, my poker-playing friend." She stood looking at him for a moment. Her hand was still up, but she had stopped waving.

It was at that moment that both she and Jim knew that their paths would never cross again. It was at that moment that they both pretended they would meet again, though they both knew this was good-bye. They refused to say good-bye; they refused to do anything about it. He could never see her buying yellow curtains for the kitchen. She could never see him mowing the lawn. They had developed what seemed to be a profoundly deep connection without many words or meaningful thoughts exchanged. They had touched each other in a way that was very important to both of them on that night, at that point in their existence. In the Middle Ages, this would have been deemed a "good day to die." In this era, and at their age, it was time to depart.

• • •

Still, for a moment, Jim closed his eyes and saw her curled up and sleeping under a blue blanket, her eyes looking beautiful in repose. Her face was calm. Her chest barely moved as she slept.

●　●　●

It was the memory of that special night and this angelic vision he decided to revisit one more time as he drank the last gulp of the beer before him. It had taken place so long ago; everyone was still alive then. The world was old and they were young. None of those statements were true any longer.

The music had become insufferably loud, and Jim was roused from his reverie by the thumping bass and the screaming throng.

Moses and the Dying Flock was playing on the jukebox again. It seemed like they were on every Friday. Athletic young men with spiked hair, polyester shirts, and baggy pants that hung low were jumping up and down. They held a cell phone in one hand and a PDA in the other. They were calling people they didn't know and sending messages to people they couldn't see. Screaming to each other about nothing, they drank wine and designer vodka with fruit juice. The girls all had body art and piercings and eyes lined in black. The orange and yellow spotlights were rotating, and the room's temperature was being raised by the frenetic energy of youth.

Jim turned for a moment and looked around him. It had gotten late early at the Glocca Morra tonight, and he wondered at the crowd. He was somewhat amazed that he didn't notice them all come in. He shook his head and looked at the empty beer glass before him. Stale white foam ran down its sides. For a moment, Jim's eyes tracked the foam as it moved slowly toward the bottom of the glass.

The barkeep tapped the bar in front of him. Trying not to compete with the din, he motioned to Jim, asking if he'd like another beer. Jim looked at the youthful crowd around him for a moment and found nothing that appealed to him. He slowly shook his head. He left a few bucks on the bar and moved towards the door. He still didn't believe that he hadn't heard all those kids come in. On some level, this concerned him. Then Jim remembered why he had come to The Gloch today. Mikey was dead. He couldn't believe it. The dreams always came strong when Jim heard of another friend dying. He tucked his flannel shirt into his jeans and approached the door. For a moment, he paused again. He shook his head. He rubbed his bloodshot eyes. Mikey was dead.

The door burst open, just barely missing Jim's head. Four high-spirited youths blasted by him on their way to the bar, laughing at the fact that they had almost run him down.

Jim walked out onto the streets of the city. It was cool outside. He looked back at the large window into The Gloch. A trick of lighting, reflection, and refraction allowed Jim to see himself in the bar, looking out and surrounded by the thumping bass speakers and the jumping kids. He knew he didn't belong there. He began to walk down the street.

One of the kids took the earbud out of his ear and ordered his drink from the barman. "What's with the old dude, man? We almost killed him coming in. Doesn't he know that this is a kid's place?"

The barman could barely hear the question, but he got the gist of what the kid was saying. "He don't hurt nobody. He comes in here every day for a beer or two and then he goes home. He seems okay, but he doesn't say much."

The kid had already replaced the earbud and turned from the barman without waiting for an answer. His world was filled with rhetorical questions because no one cared enough about the question or the answer. The barman waved the kid off.

The kid was already jumping, bumping, and grinding with a girl who wore a tight shirt that rode up her back whenever she moved. She had a blue-green tattoo just over her butt that was a large design of arrows and flourishes with the words "Seeds of Hell" above it. They were having a great time already.

Taxicabs blew by Jim as he walked. The streetlights glowed a phosphorescent blue. Everyone was rushing somewhere else and Jim was heading home. Was it a small tear or a twinkle in Jim's eye as he thought, "Hey…blue and blew…that's a homonym." Jim smiled grimly and walked home alone.

Hazen's Notch

Mary Miller had lived in Hazen's Notch all of her life. The Cold Hollow Mountains were always to the west. The Green Mountains were always to the south. Jay's Peak was always up north. The Lowell Mountains were always in the east. The Missisquoi River was never too far away. Her family always shopped in Hectorville or Lowell. Canada was always there. The sun rose in the east and set in the west. Summers were short. Winter was cold and snowy.

Mary's daddy had a farm. His daddy had the same farm before him. As a little girl, she played there with her brothers and sisters. Sometimes, they'd walk to a neighbor's farm and play with those kids. On the Fourth of July, one of the local farmers would have a big barbecue and twelve or fifteen kids would be there. Mary always enjoyed the Fourth.

Her parents took care of her schooling through the sixth grade. They needed her at home to help with the chores, and there were not enough local kids to necessitate the building of a school. After sixth grade, she went to the Catholic school with her brothers and sisters. The Catholic school taught all the tough subjects like trigonometry and algebra, subjects that seemed just plain useless to the farm kids. Nevertheless, they attended regularly to please their parents.

There was also something special about the church, with its big white steeple and the unwavering powers of motivation and intimidation exhibited by the nuns that drove the children to try to be perfect students. Sometimes, as she approached the school and church, Mary would think that God Himself had built Vermont and this powerful church with its clean white steeple because it was a place that existed with effortless perfection and a natural integrity that blended seamlessly with the beauty of the nature that surrounded it.

Mary loved Hazen's Notch. The people were always friendly and the land was magnificent. She'd walk alone on summer afternoons and notice the beauty of all the green trees, great stones, and rapidly moving streams that surrounded her. She'd track deer and other small animals and stand thrilled and amazed when she would catch up to them. The moment would break, and the deer would run deeper into the forest. She would try to follow and track again without success. It was the evanescence of nature that drove her to a greater appreciation of all the beauty that surrounded her.

In summertime, Mary would pick strawberries, and her Mama would make her favorite—strawberry jam. Winter brought heavy snows and homemade ice cream consumed before the roaring fires that Daddy built every night. Christmas meant going out to the "back forty" with the family to pick the perfect tree. Sometimes, they would have silly arguments about the quality of the trees. Sometimes, the whole family would lie back and make angels in the snow. They'd laugh and look up at the billions of stars that looked back down at them from above. When a neighbor was sick, Mary would ride with her mama to help take care of their house, their farm, or their kids. They would bring plates of food so that there would be no need for anyone to bother cooking.

They loved to help their neighbors. If there was a death in the community, it was Mary's responsibility to pick wildflowers from the fields and bring them over to the grieving family. Mary was the oldest, and her parents relied on her for most everything.

Mary had just turned twenty, and she was a little bit worried. She still had not found a husband. The only kisses she had received had been on her cheek. The only boys who had seen her undressed were her brothers, who had sneaked into the bathroom when she was seven to watch her take a bath. Her father had given them both the strap for that.

At any rate, Mary was beginning to wonder about

her future. At twenty, Rosie Tiernan had three kids. Mary wanted to be with a man. Mary wanted to be married. Mary wanted to have children and continue the same beautiful traditions with which she had grown up. Her problem was that there were no eligible males her age living in Hazen's Notch.

Mary had been mulling over her life in Hazen's Notch for a few months. She loved her family. She loved her house. She loved the Notch. Still, she was looking for something more. She wanted to know what it would be like to visit (or even live in!) a big city. She would have paid to go to St. Alban's or Swanton. She would have killed to see Burlington. Bright lights, crowded stores filled with products she had never seen before, different people on every corner—this all seemed like it would be heaven on earth to her.

After six months of wondering what city life would be like, she decided to see for herself. She told her mother that she was going to go camping on Jay's Peak and that she would be back in a few days. She actually hoped to get beyond Jay's Peak and visit Newport (which was a city big enough to satisfy her curiosity). She walked slowly, almost hesitantly, as she left for Jay's Peak. She had never lied to her mother before, and she was not so sure that she wanted to start now. She wanted to wander onto the high wire, but only if there was a safety net beneath her.

Today was Ray Stark's birthday. He had just turned

forty. He tilted his white hat down over his eyes and wiped the back of his neck with a sweat-soaked handkerchief. He looked at the handkerchief with disgust and stuck it into his white trouser pocket. He couldn't think of a single person with whom he'd want to spend his birthday.

He had just left the last bunch of sleazy acquaintances at a country fair in a Canadian border town. He had been a barker at that traveling con game for too long. It had been one of those fleabag carnivals that pay off local parishes so that they can fleece their flocks. "Throw a quarter on the plate and win a prize," he would cry on Tuesdays. Of course, these ceramic plates were covered with more grease than glaze. On Wednesdays, he'd urge the congregation to "Shoot a basket and win a prize. Three shots for a quarter." All the Vaseline in the world could not have gotten those basketballs through the hoops on the wall.

Ray was always afraid that the basketball would balance on the hoop again, like it did in Buffalo. That could have been serious trouble. He told the rube that he had made a mistake, overinflated the balls he did. He gave him a stuffed dog and moved him to another booth. It amazed him that little stuffed rags gave so many suckers so much enjoyment because they had "won" them.

The road was getting to Ray. He needed a place to settle down, a place from which he wouldn't have to move after a month or two. He had heard that a shark never backs up, that a shark must always move forward to live. He was beginning to feel like that shark, and he didn't like it.

Ray was tired. He was tired of walking. He was tired of the con game. He was tired of swindling people even though he didn't like them very much. He was tired of most everything in his life. He had to get away—maybe it was time to make a new start. At forty, he felt that he had now attained a benchmark age, an excuse for a change of life. He had spent his entire life searching for himself, yet found nothing. The only truth that he had discovered was that no one else cared.

He looked up at Jay's Peak. Maybe the hills would help him find the best part of himself. He knew that he had nowhere else to go. Ever since he was a little kid, people told him that, given time and effort, he would be all that he wanted to be. Of course, this was a blatant lie. It took something more than time and effort. Ray had given life his greatest effort, and he thought he had given it quite enough time. He had not gotten anywhere.

Ray always found it was difficult to have faith when nothing was certain. At times, he felt like a child learning to walk. To others, it was quite clear that the child could walk, but to the child, it was still an adventure with an uncertain ending. To Ray, the problem was not walking, but realizing that walking was a worthwhile endeavor to pursue. He feared that every step he had ever taken was a mistake.

Now, Ray found himself in a place where he had least expected to be; he had turned to the mountains. He came to talk to the trees because he felt that they would not talk back. Still, he was uneasy in this natural setting. He always thought that if there was a God, He probably lived away from the decadence and decay of people grouped together in cities. He was not anxious to meet God just yet. He was not sure that he ever wanted to meet God at all. He was not quite sure that God would accept him as a worthwhile specimen of man.

Right now, there were other things in nature that were far more treacherous to him than God—like porcupines, raccoons, and squirrels. Ray was not at all interested in meeting anything in its natural habitat. He was quite comfortable discussing nonsense with some drunken bimbo in a redneck bar, or telling stupid jokes to some inebriated biker urinating by a tree, but every noise on the mountaintop that night put fear into his heart. He did not know where he was or what in the world surrounded him. He did know that it was his birthday and that he was as happy as he had been in years.

Mary camped on a bed of pine needles below a large fir tree. The soft aroma of the pine, mingled with the gentle noise of the night, comforted her as she went to sleep. She was happy to be camping alone. She felt as though she was nestled in the cradle of God Himself and that the chorus of the saints was singing nature's lullaby as she fell asleep.

She looked forward to her city visit the next day. There is a certain excitement that one feels the first time he or she breaks a rule. There is the decision to change one's approach to life that, in itself, is layered with all manner of feelings that having nothing to do with the outcome of the action. There is guilt, or the lack of it; there is uncertainty or absolute certitude; but mostly, there is a question that everyone asks consciously or unconsciously as they approach the unknown. It was the question that was plaguing Mary that night and causing her great concern as she approached her sojourn to the city tomorrow. Would she ever be the same person again? She had now lied to her mama. Tomorrow she was seeing the city on her terms and for the first time. Would she love it or would she hate it? How would she ever deal with Mama if she decided that she loved it? It was incredibly exciting to Mary, but she did not approach this journey without a little bit of misgiving in her heart.

The dew was thick that night, and Ray had trouble getting up the next morning. His back ached, his head hurt, his bones were cold. Slowly, he pushed himself from the ground and wondered how he ever got there.

This was not the first time that bourbon or scotch had put him somewhere he had never expected to be. The last thing he remembered from the previous night was being rude to some overweight, drunken older woman. He thought that he had told her that it was his birthday and that he expected some sort of sexual gift which she was either incapable of or unwilling to dispense that evening. Ray laughed to himself. It had been another crazy night at life's corral, and he had lived to tell about it.

He had no idea what made him come to the mountains or how he ever survived the evening in the wild. Guys like Ray always saw danger in natural settings, yet never saw any problem with their unnatural lack of concern for all the actions and activities they undertook when inebriated. As far as Ray was concerned, he had risked the wrath of the wild the night before and survived; he did not want to take such a risk again. He knew that he had spent another night outside his habitat. He also knew that one could do this just so often without retribution from Mother Nature. She would not tolerate men like Ray, and he knew it. She wanted men like Adam in her garden and no others. He did a slow 360 as he looked for nature's protectors and predators.

He rubbed his eyes, his back, and his head and tried to figure out where he was going to go next. He knew what he was going to do. He was going to survive the day, find some cash or rich old woman, get drunk, and sleep late tomorrow. He hoped that sleep would be inside tonight.

Mary wiped the dew from her eyes and gently kissed her moist fingers. Her mother had always told her that dew was the holy water of God which was given to things wild in the evening as they rested from their daytime labors. She woke with a sweet smile on her face and a slight twinkle in her eyes. She hoped to see a small deer or other animal with which she could share the beautiful dawn. She picked mint leaves from the ground and licked them as she had done since her childhood. She laughed when she thought of the look on her brother's face when he had thought he had picked mint leaves to lick and actually picked poison sumac. He suffered for weeks.

Mary looked at the natural beauty that surrounded her. There must have been at least thirty shades of green mingled with the bright blue of the stream. It seemed as though she could see the same hues and sights forever and still marvel at their beauty. There was a certain old world constancy in nature that made her feel a part of some greater whole beyond the present moment. She rolled up her sleeping bag and started a small fire for coffee.

Ray thought he smelled something burning. His eyes began to scour the hillside for some trace of fire. He was not overly concerned about the death of the trees, the animals, or the decimation of the hillside; mostly, Ray was worried about Ray. He had heard that forest fires spread faster than men could run, so he was not going to take any chances. Finally, he thought he saw a blue wisp of smoke on the other side of the hill. It didn't appear to be a raging forest fire, so Ray thought it safe enough to approach.

As he got closer, Ray thought he smelled the unmistakable odor of coffee (nectar of the Gods for one as hungover as he) intermingled with a light smell of pine. It was a smell that later stayed etched in his mind as a reminder of this day, much like the smell of burning leaves reminded him of autumn as a child. The season was always "fall" until he smelled those burning leaves, then "autumn" had arrived. Ray had a grifter's interest in the coffee until he saw the cook. Whether it was the wondrous smell of coffee and pine to a man who knew nothing better than stale beer and wine, or the beauty of the day and its surroundings which had gone unnoticed until now, Ray was surely and swiftly taken by the cook who crouched before the fire.

She wore tailored blue jeans, which were turned up in a cuff over the tops of her construction boots. Her flannel shirt was open to the waist, and she wore a black leotard underneath. Her hair was pulled back in a sort of ponytail that Ray could only describe as a "flip" because he knew nothing of hair, its decorations, or code words. The hair color was what struck him most. He felt that he finally understood what strawberry blonde meant, and he was glad. Her eyes were a pale cool blue, like a summer sky. Her smile was absolutely perfect. Her eyebrows were just a little darker than the rest of her hair, and that only made this vision more real, more true, more beautiful to behold. He had seen many birds don outrageous plumage to attract men before, but he had never seen something so simply beautiful in all of his life.

The sight of Ray startled Mary. She knew of a lot of inbred creatures who roamed the hills, and while she didn't like them, they were usually pretty harmless. Still, she knew she was near enough to the city to be a victim to some lost and wandering deviant, so she kept her guard up. This one was certainly unkempt. The suit he was wearing must have been white once, but the wear and tear of use without laundry had the color leaning more towards beige and gray. He was wearing a businessman's hat that no self-respecting mountain man would ever wear, and his shoes were etched and designed like they had just come from the shelf of Bloomingdale's or someplace like that. His tie was loosened and pointing toward magnetic north rather than true north. His shirt was fastened with cuff links. This was not a local man.

The stranger smiled nicely and tipped his hat. He asked Mary if she had some extra coffee. He seemed somewhat slippery to her, like an eel just yanked out of the water. But he also seemed to be almost as ill at ease as she was, so she invited him to sit down. She made him a cup of coffee, and they began to talk.

He told her that he was a city boy, or at least that was the way he felt today. He had spent all of his adult life chasing dreams in cities all over the United States and

Canada. He had seen a lot of things in his day, knew a lot of people, been a lot of places. At various points in his narrative, he would pause, slowly shake his head, and look down at the ground as if it would tell him something else that he had done. While he did go on about himself, he didn't look all that proud to Mary. Mostly, he would just laugh and shake his head. She pitied this strange big city man, and she thought it was time to tell him so.

"I don't know anything about the city," she began. "I don't know anything about city ways, city people, or the things people do there. I do know some very successful farmers, though. I know men who have worked the land well and gotten great returns. I never heard any of those men speak like you. They always speak of too little rain or too much sun, eroding soil or early frost which kept their crop from being perfect. I always thought that these were silly men. Sometimes I thought they were just plain liars who didn't know how to quietly accept the great rewards that God had given them. But now I understand them as men who were looking for something—something more. A better crop gave them something to live for, something to work for. It is not clear to me what a man like you needs. You ask for so little. You seem to live for so little. What makes you happy?"

Ray's eyes were slowly diverted from the ground and into the pale cold blueness of Mary's eyes, and he was once more taken by the beauty of her face. She seemed to be genuinely mystified by him and all that he had told her. Usually his stock stories drew different reactions from people. They were either amused, confused, or disappointed by the quality, or lack thereof, of his tales. Others just dismissed him as some sort of lost wanderer and teller of strange tales.

Mary seemed genuinely concerned and pained by what he thought were light and airy tales of the fantastic dreamland that he believed his life to be. She had never seen any of the places he described, so she could not fill in the blanks with her own recollections or the false nods of the great pretending populace with whom Ray was used to dealing.

She asked him direct questions, and he had to find a way to answer them as directly as he could. He had never liked anyone enough to respect them; yet, this early morning beneath the pines, he was beginning to rediscover feelings he thought were long dead, if, indeed, they had ever existed at all.

"What would make me happy?" Ray laughed his self-deprecating laugh. "Jesus, I gave up thinking about that a long time ago. I guess I dreamed too many dreams as a kid. I wanted a happy home life with Becky Sue or Mary Lee, the beauty queen, giving me four healthy kids in the white plank board house with the red shutters. Christmas would be a happy, tearful occasion with all the family going to church, praying for each other, coming home to eggnog and open present time. Drinking beer with Fred, the neighbor, and watching my son, Walter, hit the winning home run in the Little League game. Eating Grandma's pudding on Thanksgiving. Loving my wife till the day I die. Watching my life blossom like a summer rose on a long, strong vine that would never fail in its seed or in its blossom. That's what it was all supposed to be. That's the way it's written in all the good books. I never realized that everything that is public knowledge is absolute bullshit. Life is like a beautifully painted rocking horse with rotten timbers that collapse as soon as someone sits on it."

Ray laughed again. He looked into Mary's beautiful face once again. "I guess I haven't answered your question yet. A beautiful woman, such as yourself, deserves a proper answer. Today, right now, and for the rest of my life, I'd be real happy if I knew that someone cared. That's all it would take. If I knew that there was someone, somewhere, who would care about the fact that I've spent so many nights not remembering what the hell happened because I didn't care what the hell happened. I guess I'd care more if I knew that someone else did. Ah shit, it doesn't matter that much anyway, does it? I can walk. I can talk. I can see and I can hear. What more does any man need? Maybe I don't deserve much more. I had my shot at life, I blew it."

Mary appeared to be angry at Ray's last remark. She had only known this grifter for a very short time, but she looked at him as a person who needed to be saved from himself. She had seen many old drunks in Hazen's Notch saved by the preacher. She tried to remember everything she had ever seen the preacher do. She had to build up his self-respect and move him out of his mood.

"I may not know you," she began, "but I know what I see before me now, and I don't like it. You are much more important than you think you are."

Ray laughed. "Oh, really? To who?"

Mary wasn't ready to be challenged yet, and she hesitated. "Well…to your family, your relatives. They might not see you anymore, but they do care in their hearts, and you should know that."

Ray laughed again. "My brother and I haven't spoken in twenty-five years. My mother walked out on me when I was ten or twelve, and my father before that. It's hard to keep dates straight when they both do that to you so young. They all left. I don't know when exactly. My relatives haven't spoken to each other or to me in years. We ain't real close-knit." Ray looked at the ground and did that laugh of his again.

Mary was becoming flustered and frustrated. It seemed like this man had some awful answer to any question she might ask. She wondered why she should bother. Maybe Ray didn't want help at all. Why should she waste her time? It was her upbringing, and she knew it. Her mother had always taught her to do the right thing for people and the right thing would happen for you. This man needed a different kind of help than any other man she had encountered, but he needed help just the same. She decided to tell Ray exactly what she felt rather than playing the preacher.

"I think you are a man who is in an awful lot of trouble and doesn't realize it. I feel that I could probably help you if you let me. I'm not convinced that you want help, though. I have a funny feeling you enjoy your self-pity." Mary's eyes began to tear as she finished her statement. Never in her life had she been so open, honest, and direct with anyone, let alone a perfect stranger. She was using everything she ever knew or learned. She was forming her own opinion about an important issue. Finally, Mama was not standing at the screen door; Daddy was not watching from the fields. She felt like she was in the city, on her own, and she had not yet even left the mountains. She was in paradise. She had the best of both worlds.

Ray looked at Mary and saw everything he had ever loved in any woman. He also saw one quality he had long forgotten: He hadn't seen sincerity in years. He saw it in Mary's eyes. Why should she care about him?

For one who could see, years of nonsensical nights in crowded, smoky barrooms seemed to melt away from the corners of his eyes. A few lines disappeared from his forehead, and the gray at his temples looked distinguished. A smile creased his face. He had spent so many years laughing that he had forgotten what it was to smile a smile of recognition. His head nodded slightly.

"Maybe you are right, little lady."

He smiled his charming smile. "But, hey, why don't we take a little walk so you can tell me something about this area here. Enough of the heavy talk for a while, okay? You must be from around here. Tell me about it."

Mary was a little hesitant to end their discussion so abruptly, but she saw no harm in coming back to it later. It was becoming a very beautiful day, and she thought it might do Ray good to see the countryside. A man so wrapped up in the city needs a break every once in a while.

Mary showed Ray every beautiful thing she knew in the area. They laughed and they talked and they looked at each other a lot. Ray told more tales of the city, and Mary never tired of hearing them. Once or twice, she asked him if he would be her city guide tomorrow, just as she had been his country guide today. Each time, he said yes, but the answer was never very convincing.

As the sun set, Mary and Ray watched from a mountaintop. Ray's attention was divided between the setting sun and Mary. Once or twice she caught him staring at her. She'd smile and become uneasy, wondering what she would do if Ray tried to kiss her. God, how she wanted him to try.

Finally, Ray became serious again. He spoke words to Mary that he had spoken to many women before but never meant. He knew that he finally meant the words this time. Mary was overcome by the emotions of a previously unemotional man. She had never heard such words before. She was taken by this city man and saw love and all happiness in the sun as it set over the distant city.

Ray was out of control. He had never heard himself say such things with honesty, nor had he ever seen someone as perfect and simply beautiful as Mary. For the first time in his life, he understood the torment of Eve and her life in Paradise. He had never bothered to think of such things before. Mary had brought him to this. Ray, like Eve, could not leave the fruit on the tree to rot and die. Nor could he let the beautiful fruit fall to the ground to be bruised and useless forever. Like Eve, he felt the need to consume it, even if it meant leaving Paradise forever. No one actually wants to see Paradise fall or beauty fade.

He knew that what he was about to do was for Mary's benefit. He pulled his revolver from his belt and shot her. He knew that there were no happy endings. He left the mountaintop. He did not turn around.

Mary's body was found eventually. It had become badly decomposed on the mountainside. Everyone in Hazen's Notch said it was a senseless killing. Ray knew better.

The Gathering Tree

I am nothing more than a sordid mediocrity. My life's work is nothing more than a vanity. My life is a testament to the failures of men." As the pastor's speech slowed, his demeanor changed. The life he had brought to the early portions of this jeremiad had been dulled, its edges softened by a long examination of his failures that now had been transformed into a hopeless dirge. To some, the priest's speech had descended to nothing more than repetitious drivel.

The fire, which began as a spark of flint over dry leaves, was now roaring. The priest had spent the afternoon carrying his books and possessions to the site. As he spoke about his earthly failures, he tossed more and more items into the flames. The crowd, which had started as a small stream of close friends, had grown to a flood that surrounded the hillside upon which the priest spoke. Most were attracted to the large fire, but some had come at the priest's behest. For weeks, he had been putting up notices on trees in the surrounding villages announcing his sermon on "The Never-Ending Depravity and Mediocrity of Mankind." It was a sentiment to which anyone with good Calvin blood could easily relate.

On the hilltop, beside the great fire, a small sapling grew. It was said to have been planted by the Indians after a great council fire. It was said that the Indians wanted a "council tree," a place where great tribal events could be held and tribal disputes discussed and resolved. The townsfolk knew this because, in battle, a small group of braves had retreated to this hill and circled around the sapling to protect it.

The tree was described by the Indians with great reverence. "This tree is fed by the same earth that feeds us," they said. "This tree is the plant most sacred in the forest. It will draw its strength from all that is around it, and share that strength with all who respect it."

The townsfolk laughed at the Indian braves and shot them where they stood.

The sapling seemed so small and insignificant that no one bothered to destroy it. Besides, some of the town's warriors wanted to mark the site of this great battle for years to come. To them, a growing sapling on this hilltop location seemed suitable. They let it grow.

The pastor's fire was growing quite strong, and the young tree was now in danger. At the height of his enthusiasm, the pastor asked others to cast aside useless articles of this world and feed his fire to end all depravity. Some of the townsfolk, who had been swept up in the sea of the priest's chimera, joined in.

The pastor's frenzy was growing as he looked into the faces of the townspeople in the flickering light. Finally, his gaze fell upon a woman named Hannah, a woman he secretly coveted. She smiled at him. He stared at her face, and then his eyes fell to her breasts. For a moment, his sermon stopped. Perfection, they were. Perfection, she was; and yet, he knew there was imperfection in her being and in her life. Why would he worship an imperfect god? Why would he fall prey to the base world of man's love for the simple and the bestial?

The pastor ripped off his topcoat and tossed it onto the fire. Then, he tossed his shirt in after it and stood barechested before the shocked townspeople. The pastor had reached a new height of emotional fervor brought on by the presence of one he privately loved.

"I can never lead. I cannot be your guide. My life has been spent pretending to know, pretending to be, attempting to live without striving for perfection. I have not been a proper servant of God. I can never win the kingdom of heaven; I can only pretend to win. I can never be; I can only pretend to be." He screamed in agony, took off the rest of his clothing, and threw it onto the fire. He stood before the community naked and crying, begging for God's forgiveness. Some women screamed and scurried away with their children. Others fell to their knees and prayed to God to forgive their troubled pastor. Hannah rushed to the pastor's side, took off her coat, and wrapped it around him. She held him close and kissed his neck.

"You are a great man," she whispered. "Come, now; let us leave this haunted hill. Come with me. I will take care of you." Her hands caressed his back as she spoke.

The pastor stared wildly at Hannah. "Wretch," he screamed as he grasped her breasts and pushed her away. The coat fell to the ground and he stood naked once again. "Wretched am I! Wretched are you! Join me as I cleanse myself in the earthly hellfire that consumes all depravity."

The pastor turned and leapt into the fire. His final screams of agony were heard from the hilltop by the many who had already retreated, while others stood in stony silence, horrified by what they had just witnessed, wondering what it all meant.

Two farmers stood on a small berm not far from the pastor's pyre. They had been smoking their pipes and watching the proceedings in silence. When the pastor cast himself into the fire, one of the farmers gasped. Instinctively, he moved to save the pastor. His friend reached out and grasped his arm to stop him as the sound of the pastor's screams filled the hilltop. Confused by the actions of his companion, the farmer was torn between his instinct to help and what he knew to be the wise admonition of his friend. The screams of the pastor slowly receded to an eerie wail and then it was over.

The farmer stood staring at the pyre which now contained the dead man and all of his life's work. His eyes began to tear. He felt like there was nothing to say. His mind was racing, and he was trying to control it. He tried to make sense of the speech he had just heard and the irrational actions of the pastor which he had just witnessed. Finally, he spoke as he stared at the fire. "Quite a zealot, he was. Quite a zealot." He hated himself for saying something so obvious and so simple.

The other farmer moved his gaze from the fire as he spoke to his friend. "Zealots aren't always right. Passion can speak louder than truth, but that doesn't mean it's greater than truth. Problem is that sometimes the volume of passion can overpower truth, and bad things happen."

The farmer didn't know what to say. This reaction was cold even for a man as calculating as Josiah. Yet, Josiah was his best friend and he didn't want to hurt him, so he decided to use his favorite conversation stopper until he could figure out what to say next. "Yup, guess so." He nodded and stuck his pipe back in his mouth. They both smoked as the townspeople moved to extinguish the fire.

The farmer reengaged the eyes of his friend. "You can't take this too lightly, Josiah. You shouldn't dismiss the man before us. He seems foolish now, seems to be a man beyond saving, so why bother trying? But don't dismiss the life. The pastor tried to help us all the time. True, he was a bit short on the skills of salvation and a bit long on passion and zeal. But he always wanted to help."

Josiah harrumphed at his good friend's comment, and his eyes twinkled before they formed a squint so tight that it seemed as if it were set in cement. "I think we all saw the passion and zeal he had for dear Hannah. It didn't seem right to me. Did that seem right to you?"

"Of course not, Josiah. You know that I was not speaking about that. Passion and zeal force reason aside every time and allow tragedy to enter a situation unencumbered. Irrational exuberance, an unfettered mind, a situation half-examined—all these things can lead to the death of reason and the end of all things good. Mourn not the pastor if that is what you choose to do, but I will say a quiet prayer that this town, these people, and this hilltop will never witness the death of reason ever again."

Josiah was a cantankerous man who appreciated his own stubborn ways much more than the people who existed around him did. He could see the virtue of his dear friend's argument but refused to accede to it publicly. "I am a farmer, my friend. I have no great dreams for these people, this town, the hilltop, or the smoldering pastor before us. It is my duty to fight frost as winter approaches and drought in midsummer; I am a good man who will continue to do good because I know what is right. I have neither the time nor the inclination to do the same for another human being whose business is not mine."

A certain sadness crept into the eyes of Josiah's friend as he realized the lonely place that Josiah had chosen to live his life. He wanted their argument to end without further confrontation; he felt the discussion had taken a turn too heated already. He smiled slightly and touched Josiah on the shoulder as he spoke to him. "I see your point my friend. I see your point. Let's leave this place. Our workday begins early tomorrow."

• • •

For many years, nothing would grow in the area of the hill where the fire had burned the hottest. The hill came to be known as Scar Hill because, from a distance, it looked like a big, black wound had been branded into the greenery of the hill.

As the towns surrounding the hilltop grew, the encounter on Scar Hill became a legend that was repeated to eager listeners and embellished over time. Eventually, the story was relegated to the classification of town myth or old lore by those who felt the lessons of the evening were inappropriate to their agenda.

Hannah never left the town. She had been horribly embarrassed by the events of that terrible evening and lived her life in total seclusion. She died in her small, unadorned house alone. Although Hannah's life had been destroyed by the events of that evening, the sapling had survived and was now a tall tree of many winters. Its long branches extended far from the trunk. In summer, it was home to nests of bobolinks. In winter, it stood like an old gray man with its great arms extended, welcoming people to the hill and, by extension, to the small towns that grew around it.

Young ladies with white flowing dresses would sit upon Scar Hill under the arms of the old tree reading poetry and fiction, discussing secret and not-so-secret loves. Often, they were accompanied by young men cautiously approaching their first forays into love and, sometimes, rejection. Children from the surrounding villages would meet on the hill and under the tree because it was the focal point of the communities that surrounded Scar Hill. They would create great fantasies about their place in history and how they would have saved some damsel in distress, or the town itself, from unspeakable evil by fighting the wars of Scar Hill.

Summer nights saw the tree surrounded by small blankets upon the hill as young lovers lay under its boughs and discovered reasons to love and to share sentiments that ran strong in the canyons of their minds. Magical thinking became the order of the evening as each loving couple who knew nothing about love plotted their futures and anticipated great joys and successes. Soft breezes shook the boughs of the old tree slightly and, when the evenings were moon bright, shifting patterns of darkness and light flowed across the lovers' faces. The tree grew taller, the trunk grew wider, the population shifted from decade to decade, yet they always returned to the tree on Scar Hill.

• • •

Rene Millet always hated his name. As a child, he was mocked by others with more conventional names. He became quiet and introspective, afraid to share his ideas about things because they would never be accepted. He'd grown up in one of the towns that surrounded Scar Hill.

As a boy, he often climbed Scar Hill with his brothers and sisters. Sometimes, in winter, when there was enough snow, they would sled down the least populated side of the hill. Rene did not care for his life, but he loved Scar Hill and the great tree that grew upon it. He was barely a teenager when he took Claire, his first girlfriend, up the hill and under the tree for a "talk." To Claire and Rene, it sometimes felt like that date had occurred many, many years before, though it had not been so long ago. For years they sat upon that hill together, laughing and gently touching each other as they exchanged ideas and opinions both great and small.

As Claire sat beside Rene, surveying the others on the hill and the towns of the valley below, she said, "'Scar Hill' is too harsh a name for this place, don't you think? For so many years, so many people have enjoyed this hill and sat beneath this beautiful tree—we need to rename this spot." Her eyes glistened as she stared at Rene. Her legs were crossed at the ankle, and she leaned back on her hands as she spoke.

Rene saw something completely different. The light of the sun was reflected in her blue eyes. The absolute beauty of youth was shown in the light red blush in her cheeks. Her body was perfectly contoured and proportioned. Her thoughts were well connected and eloquently communicated. At that moment, Rene realized that he was in love.

The old tree had heard it all before. The old tree had seen it all before. The boughs swayed gently in the slight breeze. Rene felt the magic in the air; he saw the transcendent beauty in Claire's face and manner. He wanted to reach over and touch her, but he was afraid that others on the hillside might laugh and make fun.

"The name has existed for centuries now. It ties the history of these towns to this beautiful place. How can we rename it? What would we call it?"

Claire's hands reached over to stroke Rene's as she spoke. "My darling, Scar Hill is a name associated with pain and darkness. People come here not only for the view of the valley. They come to get together beneath this beautiful old tree that has seen everything and been here for everyone. Instead of Scar Hill, why not call it the Gathering Tree, a place where all will meet and love and live forever?" She grasped Rene's hand tightly as she spoke.

Rene paused to consider Claire one more time. He knew that he loved her; he just wanted to know why. She was funny and witty, beautiful and kind; those things were all given. But she also loved him, his thoughts, his deeds, his jokes—and his weaknesses. Rene was certain that the love he felt would last forever. "The Gathering Tree it is, then." Without thinking, he placed his hand over hers.

Rene loved the concept of a Gathering Tree that pulled the disparate worlds and lives of disparate times and ages together. A great unifier, he thought, not a damaged hill. "From now on, we will not refer to this place as Scar Hill. Henceforward, we visit the Gathering Tree." He took out his penknife and carved C+R on the tree.

Rene and Claire got married beneath the Gathering Tree. Slowly, the people in the surrounding towns adopted the new name, and "Scar Hill" faded into the hazy ambiguity of times past. For those who remembered, it seemed that the old black scar had finally been covered entirely by green.

Rene became a successful man of business. His company was based upon the ability to make disparate businesses communicate better. He named the company after The Gathering Tree. Its logo was the large, ubiquitous tree that sat upon a hill with a tiny C+R etched across its trunk. It made Rene smile whenever he saw it. It was the one thing in his life that always reminded him of Claire and the lovely beauty of their youth.

The Gathering Tree acquired more companies as it became more successful. As it grew, the name was dropped, and only the symbol of the large tree remained. Rene and Claire became quite rich. Every Sunday through spring and summer, Rene and Claire would bring a blanket and sit beneath the Gathering Tree. They would still share their thoughts and secrets. They would still see life and humor in each other's eyes. They would still hold hands (when Rene found it comfortable, which had grown to be more often), and as the days ended, Rene loved to see the sunset reflected in Claire's blue eyes.

The very wide boughs of the tree now seemed to embrace the entire hilltop and the people who came there. At times, it seemed as if the tree would bend low to listen or move to allow sunlight to fall on a particularly enchanting face. The magical thinking that occurred on the hilltop was still in full view for those who knew where and how to look.

Then, one day, Rene suddenly found his company in the midst of a controversy. Some environmental zealots had grown upset with the company position on some obscure issue that was violently important to them. They did not know much about The Gathering Tree companies, but they knew that the corporate stance on this issue was unacceptable. They began to descend upon the towns in the valley like politically correct locusts, demanding that The Gathering Tree companies bend their position to conform to their point of view. They papered the towns of the valley with leaflets urging the citizens to rise up against The Gathering Tree.

When rocks were thrown through the glass doors of The Gathering Tree's offices, Claire became afraid. She asked to employ more security. The protestors hired huge buses and loaded them up with like-minded thinkers to rally in front of Rene's house and his corporate office. Mostly, they were just loud, but at times, they seemed to be potentially violent. Still, for all of their enthusiasm, their message was not being received. The townsfolk were not energized.

These folks need a wake-up call, thought one of the organizers, as he sat on the hillside one day, studying a leaflet that had been written by a fellow protestor—a blistering attack on The Gathering Tree organization.

At the top of the leaflet, The Gathering Tree logo sat in the middle of the text. He looked at the tree on the hillside and found their appearance to be remarkably similar. He had a moment of zealous inspiration.

We need to draw greater attention to our campaign, he thought. A hilltop bonfire would be just the thing. He spoke to the others, and while all were concerned with the damage that a bonfire might cause to the hillside, they felt it was a necessary casualty in the war against corporate insensitivity. The plan was in place.

That night, the protestors, armed with large cans of

gasoline, set fire to a huge pile of corporate literature and annual reports from The Gathering Tree. Their great enthusiasm about their purpose brought great joy to the project. The bonfire grew quickly. The group screamed obscenities and unintelligible generalities describing the banality and depravity of The Gathering Tree's holdings as they tossed all manner of combustibles on the tall flames. The townsfolk stood on different parts of the hilltop and struggled to make sense of what they were saying.

The protestors shouted into their bullhorns, exhorting the crowd to join their cause; yet, as the fire grew larger, the interest of the spectators began to wane. Desperate to regain the attention of the dispersing crowd, one of the protestors tossed a large can of gasoline onto the flames. There was a minor explosion that rocked the hilltop and directed all eyes to the large flames that were now beginning to consume the Gathering Tree itself. The townspeople shrieked in horror, searching desperately for water to put out the flames. There was nothing they could do; by the time the fire department arrived on the scene, the tree had been consumed by a pyre that was burning out of control.

Darkness fell deeper, and the fire was raging. The tree was gone, and the protestors were shouting for change. The townsfolk from the valley ringed the hill and its fire, and the group extended deep into the valley. All of the people stood in stunned silence, realizing that there was nothing they could do. No one had the courage to challenge the loud and aggressive zealots.

Rene and Claire stood holding hands in his office, looking at the fire upon the hill, their eyes filled with tears. There were no words to express the sadness they felt.

Finally, Claire looked at Rene. She saw the tears and the flames fighting for dominance in his eyes. He saw the vacant light of a fire framed by a black sky reflected in hers. They held each other briefly and then went home.

The next day, Rene shut the doors of The Gathering Tree forever. He planned to sell all the firm's assets and distribute the money to his employees. The closing of The Gathering Tree was great news to the protestors; they celebrated on the hilltop before they left town.

It was at sunset three days after the protest that Claire and Rene finally returned to the hill. A very large black scar ran across the hilltop. Rene looked into Claire's eyes and saw the cold, gray sunset of autumn. Claire looked at Rene and struggled mightily as she attempted to speak. Her eyes surveyed the bleak desolation of what had been her favorite place in all the world, and she felt a great weakness consume her body and her spirit. She felt withered and ancient. A wave of hopelessness, helplessness, and sorrow that began as a pain in the pit of her stomach left her body as a tsunami of tears, a cacophony of indistinct wails and uncontrolled shrieks. Rene moved to console her without success.

"Why, Rene? Why?" Claire clutched a tear-soaked handkerchief as she slammed the hillside with her hand in frustration.

"Zealots, my dear…angry zealots who believed what they believed without knowing…. They didn't know us. They didn't know this place. They didn't know this tree. It didn't matter to them that they didn't know. They only knew what they wanted to know." Rene hated himself for saying something so obvious and so simple, but such is the way of all words of consolation.

Claire's moist hand opened slightly as it rested upon the hillside. A soft zephyr from some unknown precinct blew the handkerchief a few inches away from her as she looked at Rene. Her eyes were still wet and shot red; her lip was still quivering as she endeavored to speak. Her hair was matted onto her forehead and at odd positions around her ears. Perspiration had formed at the base of her neck, and the top button of her blouse was stuck to her skin. Claire was angry and frustrated, and she felt like she had lost control of what had been the root of her existence as a woman, and their existence as a couple—she needed an explanation that she could believe in. For the first time in her life, she felt Rene's words to be lacking.

"Just because they are zealots…that does not justify their actions or opinions. They were wrong. Now trag-edy has found its way into our lives. What do we do now, Rene? Whom do we see about that?"

Rene looked briefly into her eyes and then turned to view the sunset. "We move on. We rebuild. We grow again." He pulled an old clay pipe out of the breast pocket of his coat and stuck it between his teeth. He stared at the sunset in silence.

Claire looked at her husband with great astonishment and disappointment. She stared at him for a few moments as he gazed at the sunset. Then, she folded her knees under her chin and surveyed the hillside one last time. Her handkerchief now sat beside her as she rested her arms on her knees and took her view of the sunset. A stronger wind began to blow, and the handkerchief rolled away. The tears in her eyes would not dry, and Claire suddenly realized that she had nothing else to say to Rene. This was a feeling that she could grow to hate.

Lone Wolf

It was a bright sun that illuminated the leaves on the trees in front of Ed McDowell's house that day. Ed stood by an open window watching the leaves rattle in the gusty wind that blew through the valley.

All things considered, he thought it could be classified as a "nice day." He was alone in his cabin, which was situated about five miles from the middle of nowhere, and he was fairly content. He scratched his unshaven face and ran his hand through his unkempt hair. The wind gusted, the leaves rattled, the floorboards of his cabin seemed to shake in anticipation of this lovely summer day—a quivering expectation had filled his valley. Ed shook his head and sat down in a rickety wooden chair he had bought long ago. He thought that he had a case of cabin fever. He'd been out in the country too long.

Leaving the house, and all things "inside," Ed realized that he was surrounded by what was outside—the leaves, the trees, the wind, and the valley. Even the sun, which for some reason seemed ghastly beautiful today, hung like a host afire suspended outside his home.

Things "outside" were nothing more than items in a room bigger than the one inside his cabin. The cabin and all things outside were inside his mind and always just beyond the power of his thought.

His grandson Elliot, the artist, was to visit Ed that day. Elliot dropped by infrequently, and he was always very kind, polite, and "interested." Ed shook his head in disgust. Elliot was so busy being interested in his grandfather that he forgot that sometimes an old man wanted to do nothing else but talk to another guy.

The grandson looked at his grandfather like a curiosity that kept Elliot in touch with days gone by. Elliot wanted to know all the names and the dates, the loves and the lives of those who had died. He thought that he might get an Inspiration from his grandfather—the talking tombstone.

Sometimes, Ed felt used. Elliot was always speaking of his next painting and his plans to include his grandfather somewhere in the scene. Ed grimaced at the thought. He had never been pictured anywhere in life; why should he be pictured for someone else's foolish posterity when dead? Though his paintings were quite good, Elliot never fully captured the intricacies, the nicks, cuts, and jagged edges of the original. His naïve view of art prevented him from letting "seeming be." Ed did not want to be pictured in any such painting.

Still there was no doubting that young Elliot was

polite. He was a good boy to venture out to this remote part of the country to speak to old Ed. Ed considered that Elliot must be better than most grandsons on the planet— at least he cared enough to travel to the cabin. No matter how often Elliot was infuriatingly condescending, he was there. Ed thought that it was a help. It did give him something to do. He prepared a cup of tea so that he might have something to drink before Elliot arrived, and something to fiddle with when Elliot became tedious or maddening. It was thus that Elliot found Ed when he called to him from the porch.

Ed turned slowly, smiling uneasily. His tea was not quite ready and neither was he. His arms did not fit into his shoulders, and his shoulders balanced on some wrong bones. He tried to arch his back slightly to get everything into place as he extended his hand to his grandson.

Elliot was smiling broadly, his head nodding slightly as he greeted his grandfather. He noticed Ed arching his back and thought that it was great that the old man wanted to stand tall to greet his grandson. His grandfather had not changed much since his last visit. The cabin looked about the same. Elliot was still smiling.

Ed turned to his whistling teapot and relaxed slightly. Without turning back, he asked if Elliot wanted any tea. Ed knew that Elliot would say yes even if he would choke on tea, so he removed two cups from the cupboard.

"So." Ed paused to remove his tea bag from his cup.

"What's new?" He did his best to smile over the enormous sigh he had surreptitiously let out.

The shutters flapped against the cabin as Elliot spoke.

"New? Well, I've finished another painting—the Manassa Mansion. Remember? You told me about the place the last time I was here. I wanted to paint you on a rocking chair on the front porch, but the view was too distant, and you wouldn't have been any more than a speck in the picture."

"Did it come out well?"

"Oh, yes, it sold right away. I wish I could have put you in it, though—I really do."

Ed finished his tea and thought about the Manassa house. He belonged in a rocker on the porch about as much as he belonged on a seagull's wing in springtime.

"Manassa Mansion, hmmm. I told you about that place last time?" Ed's conversations were few, but never remembered.

"Why, yes, grandfather." Elliot straightened his glasses. "Don't you remember? You told me about that large party you had there. The time you tore a whole room apart and threw it on the front lawn. The time your friends wanted to throw some bimbo out of a third-story window."

Ed chuckled slightly and ran his fingers through his hair. "I told you about that? Hmmm." He chuckled again. "Well, how did the picture come out?"

"Quite well. It sold right away."

"Ah, yes, you told me that, didn't you." Ed was talking into his hand. "Sold right away. Jerry Wook died, you know." Ed dipped his head slightly, "I thought I felt him go. It sounds strange, I know."

Elliot was concerned. He noticed, as he visited his grandfather more often, that his grandfather would mumble and often speak into his hand. Elliot wanted to draw his grandfather out of his shell. "Tell me about it, Grandfather."

"Well, it was a week ago, maybe two, when old Erias the postman came and gave me the bad news. It was a letter from Jerry's sister explaining how he had passed away."

"What did she say?"

"Well, the usual what-a-loss/good-friend/six-feet-under/never-see-again type letter. The strange thing was the way he died. He was sitting in a chair, his hands clenched on its arms, his eyes wide open, and his mouth agape in a noiseless shout. Now, I don't know if I ever told you about Jerry before, but never have I ever heard of a more fitting end."

Elliot's interest was piqued. "What was he like?"

"Jerry? Well, he was like nothing you've ever seen before. He stood with both feet on the wrong side of the double yellow line and dared the trains to hit him. He was a brilliant guy who knew just about everything, but never appeared to have a sense about what was going on.

"He used to tell me that he always saw life as a series of

photographs flashing before him. Unrelated shutters from ten million different cameras clicking in unison before his eyes. The quality of the prints, and so the quality of one's life, is always governed by others.

"Jerry would always say that most people are nothing more than mealymouthed, malevolent bureaucrats who always want to touch up the picture and foul up the sequence. Jerry didn't have much use for people, though he was a very friendly fellow.

"He said that people thought that he was a poor part in society's machine—a part that would break down and need replacing. He was determined to prove to himself that they were wrong. He grew to be irreplaceable in his friends' eyes. I don't cry often, but when I heard he died, I did.

"His eyes were always clear. His voice was always true. Nothing rattled Jerry. He took everything as it came to him. God, I admired him."

"What did he do for a living, Grandfather?"

"Huh? What?" Ed's wonderful daydreams were interrupted.

Elliot felt uncomfortable as he reiterated his question.

"He worked in a Customs House. Does it matter?" Ed was visibly annoyed. He wondered why Elliot always felt compelled to interrupt him.

"Well, uh, no." Elliot grew increasingly uncomfortable.

"Yes, I know it doesn't matter." Ed was infuriated

and far away from pleasant reverie. The shutters slammed against the house.

"How are your mother and father?" Ed's mood eased slightly as he tried to steer the conversation to the safely mundane.

"Mother is better. She seems much happier lately. Father has not changed. He still lives the Thoreauian life of quiet desperation. He struggles and succeeds in his own fashion. I think he fights too hard for too little gain. He is killing himself, you know."

"Yes, yes, and so are you when you try to put me on the porch of Manassa Mansion. You are trying to make a perfect painting; he is trying to live a life with the cards he's been dealt. There is something noble in that, don't you see? Quiet desperation? I doubt it. He lives the life which we all do—the life of relentless anticipation."

"But we can change the deck, can't we, Grandfather? Why not discard the bad cards and strive for a better hand?"

Elliot had made the mistake of interrupting again.

"Listen, boy. I said relentless anticipation. I know of a man whose plane crashed into the Northern waters in the dead of winter. Many died. It was quite tragic. There was one guy, an older gent, who swam around in the water, passing up the lifesaving efforts of the rescue team, so that others could be saved. He was throwing the life preserver that was meant for him onto the shoulders of others. Relentless anticipation." The wind gusted outside the cabin. A storm was approaching.

"And what happened to him, Grandfather?" Elliot had not heard the story before.

Ed turned to Elliot for the first time, looking him in the eye. "He died, of course. No one was ever quite sure of his identity, but he lived surely as you or I. Like us, he had been waiting for his moment, waiting to contribute, waiting for the world to turn to him for some sort of help, waiting to do something with his life. By God, he did it. That, my boy, is the way to live."

Elliot knew better than to interrupt again. His grandfather was beginning to rant. His eyes had caught fire, and his face was flushed with the light that seized his eyes. It was beginning to rain outside, and Elliot could see lightning crowning a nearby mountaintop.

His grandfather began to pace back and forth as he rubbed his beard and concocted his next outburst.

"Living." He stood staring between the raindrops. Then he laughed slightly. "Living ain't no more than having fun and keeping your head."

Ed's eyes were ablaze as he turned to stare at Elliot. He felt a surge of deep feeling pounding within his chest. "Christ, we were crazy. Jerry, me, the whole gang—we had it. We had picked the lock of the vault of creation, stepped inside, and turned the safety deposit boxes of humanity inside out."

Not seeing a hint of recognition in Elliot's eyes, Ed's attention returned to the rattling floorboards as he continued his impassioned description of his past. "Picked God's vault, we did. We were all half drunk and crazy and hit the right combination."

He slammed his kitchen table with a fully clenched fist, and Elliot jumped slightly. Ed turned his attention to the world outside. "There are so many who inherit the riches of life and are surrounded by its beauty. They walk into gold-encrusted halls, sit in red velvet chairs, and mention how beautiful it all is. They are spoiled rotten. Like an old banana, the gold has gone brown. They might as well be in some goddamn luncheonette. They glide into giant ballrooms, sit with their faces in fruit cups, clean up, and do it again at some other time in some other city."

He turned to Elliot again. "We had to try so much harder. We used up most of our magic producing the lightning of moments and didn't have the power to create the thunder and sustain the magic. We can't rattle the walls of wretched excess down. The electric eyes are always on. Society knows we are intruders. As long as we realize the same, no harm is done. After all, we are still having one hell of a time. The damndest thing is that we can accomplish all of this without anyone noticing. It just shows you how much is there." Ed smiled and stared at Elliot.

He grabbed Elliot by the shoulder and shook him slightly, to get him into the joke. He saw an uneasiness in his grandson's eyes that sickened him. Elliot reached to straighten his glasses and smiled at the unknown humor his grandfather had found in the situation. He was trying to find a point in his grandfather's speech, or at least some way to reply.

Elliot paused and looked at his watch. "I think it's time for me to leave, Grandfather. I have to paint more pictures so I can pay the rent, you know. I am not like you; I am still the struggling artist."

The rain had stopped. The storm had passed. A setting sun appeared from beneath a gray cloud in the west. The light attracted Ed's attention for a moment.

The fire passed from his eyes, and he sat down in a wicker chair. He looked at Elliot and smiled in a condescending way. He tapped Elliot's arm slightly and winked. "You're right, son. You struggling painters have got to work. You go on home now. Say hello to the family for me."

Elliot put a scarf around his neck and got up from the table. "Thanks for the tea and the talk." He was very uneasy.

Ed winked again, "Good to have you. At least that thunderstorm has passed; now you can go home safe." Ed smiled.

"Yes, I guess I won't be needing this," laughed Elliot as he produced an umbrella from his pocket.

Ed sighed. "No, I guess you won't—but I'm sure you were glad to have it."

"Yeah, well bye, Grandpa. See you soon."

"Bye, son. Good luck."

Ed turned and went into his kitchen. He looked at his old kitchen table with all its nicks and scratches. He sat in a kitchen chair for a moment and stared at the table in silence. He rose and looked out the window. He saw a bluebird on a distant branch and smiled. Now he could go to sleep and dream. That would be better. He had seen enough scratches in furniture for one day.

Connecting Thoughts

Emma was forty years old today. She sat staring out the window of her favorite bar, looking at her favorite city, happy that it was her favorite time of year. Trees were beginning to blossom; a softly massaging zephyr tossed the hair of the passersby lightly and made everyone look slightly disheveled. She appreciated that because she always felt slightly disheveled and off the mark.

Her poetry was an extension of her disheveled life. Without the rules of grammar to constrict and constrain, she was able to write and be whatever, whomever, and wherever the words took her. Her cream-colored dress hung limply off her shoulders, and the little red strawberries that covered the fabric bent at awkward angles and unattractive curves. Ever since she was a child, Emma loved strawberries. As an adult, she transferred this love of a particular fruit to the love of a particular pattern. Much of her clothing, and a few of her hats and gloves, had tiny strawberries woven into the fabric. Sometimes, when she was alone and gazing upon the strawberries, she felt warm and comfortable like a child in the cocoon of a bed with a large quilt surrounding her form. Sometimes she saw disappointment and misery in the strawberries before her. Strawberries showed Emma everything. They were the symbol of everything she was and everything she was not; everything that could have been and everything that would never be. Mostly, strawberries reminded Emma of what did not exist in her life.

Her brown sandals and wool socks were both the harbinger of early spring and the reminder that, this year, winter lingered longer than it should. Emma was depressed and confused. She was alone again on her birthday.

She thought that there was a poem in this angst, but she knew that it would never be written. Emma had trouble with her poetry. Try as she might, Emma could not reach the angst that could drive her poetry to a level more profound. She would try, she would fail, she would try again. Finally she would think it was "good enough." Emma had a problem with commitment: commitment to her craft and commitment to her life—it was all too hard, too exhausting.

Emma also had a problem with people. She didn't like them very well, and they didn't like her. A more appropriate statement might be that Emma thought that no one ever took the time to notice or know her. She interrupted her thoughts to stare at her half-finished cup of tea. She realized that she had been thinking this way for years and years. Emma grew more depressed and stared more deeply into her cup of tea.

Lini had come to America from Ireland, though her coloring and appearance spoke to a different heritage. She had been working at Sam's Bar for over two years now, and she was looking for something better. Lini was looking for a man to rescue her from this meaningless existence. She preferred good looks, personality, and depth of thought, but she would be satisfied with a man who just had money. Lini was not destitute, nor was she even poor. She had simply transcended the desire for life to be meaningful and had refocused her attention on fun. She smiled sweetly at Mac, the bartender, and asked for four more boilermakers for the suburban hausfraus at the table in the corner.

Lini's corner table customers were not her cup of tea. They were overweight, overly loud, and overbearing women of means who treated Lini as their servant rather than their waitress. Lini was relatively sure that she was serving drunks from suburbia who had done nothing in their lives other than marry well. She resented their feelings of self-importance. Worse than that, Lini knew they would sit for hours on end without leaving a tip.

"Where are the drinks, sweetie? Put a little hustle in your bustle, dear. We're thirsty!"

Marta was speaking for the group again. It was her way. She spoke loudest and told what she thought to be the funniest jokes. She rarely took the time for life's introspection that had been thrust upon Emma for almost forty years (or so Emma thought). Marta measured success in laughter and frivolity. The less serious the conversation, the less threatened she felt. When engaged in personal gossip, her voice would change. The tone would drop a few octaves, and her demeanor would adopt an air of seriousness unparalleled in her drunken peer group. Still, this seriousness was nothing more than a façade. Marta had a genuine interest in gossip, but any relation it had to substance was merely a pretense.

Marta's hair was chestnut brown and rolled tightly into permanent curls. Her joke was that she always knew what color her hair was—all she needed to do was read the side of the box. Marta thought she was very good-looking, especially for an older woman. She rarely passed a mirror without primping her hair or fixing her lipstick. She always blew herself a kiss at the end of this moment of self-examination.

The girls had come to the city for their weekly outing. Marta had founded this club some years ago, and while its membership had shifted some over the years, they always had a quorum for gossip and booze in a bar somewhere far from home.

Lini dropped the boilermakers on the table with disgust. As she deposited the last drink, she wiped the serving tray with a cloth, holding it to her breast as she returned to the bar. She leaned on the bar and deposited it atop a pile of trays that sat beside the fruit used to garnish drinks. Lini grabbed a cherry, put it into her mouth, and was about to remove the stem as the bar door slowly opened and a mildly attractive, middle-aged man entered from the sea of sunlight that washed the sidewalk outside the bar.

The man slowly surveyed the situation at the bar, seemed to mull things over, and moved a bar stool at the end of the bar far away from Lini's fixed stare. He rubbed his hands together, wiped his face for no apparent reason, and ordered a beer.

The *Daily Telegraph*'s morning edition lay on the bar by the stranger's seat. He examined the front page, smirked, shook his head from side to side, and returned the newspaper to its place on the bar. The bartender placed a beer before him, and the man drank a long, self-satisfied draught. He returned the glass to the surface of the bar, wiped his face, and slowly began to survey the room again.

Tears were streaming down Emma's cheeks. She was alone in the big city on her birthday, and there was nothing she could do about it. She had noticed the well-dressed stranger as he entered the bar. He reminded her of a man whom she had never known but always loved. He used to ride the same train as her when she was spending her time in poetry workshops at the university. He even smiled at Emma once. She had felt herself turn bright red as she redirected her stare to the floor of the train. She remembered that, even then, she never knew how to react to people who paid any attention to her. She viewed herself as a young poetess struggling with issues of life that no one else really understood. She needed the distance between her work and the citizens of the world. Without that distance, there could be no great creation. Without that distance, she would lose the perspective necessary to unearth truth everlasting. For a moment, in Sam's Bar, Emma was young again—alone with her thoughts, alone with her dreams and fantasies, reaching for that which was just beyond her capabilities, but not beyond her powers of imagination.

Emma's reverie was interrupted as she looked at her forty-year-old hands. She realized that all she had now was a life's collection of poems that no one ever read and the distance from people that she had worked so hard to attain. She had nothing left in her life but her work and her pets. Her pets were always a source of great joy and companionship. Lately, she had been growing less and less fond of her work.

She saw her countenance reflected in the windows of Sam's Bar. Her hair was an unsightly combination of mousy brown and gray. Whatever sex appeal she may have had once was now gone. She knew her dresses never fit well. She knew that wool socks with sandals would not move the man at the end of the bar in her direction. She knew that her poetry was not good enough, and yet it was all she thought about. She kept people at a distance created by her own devices, and now she was crying because people were too distant and she was alone. She wiped the tears from both cheeks, tried to compose herself, and motioned to Lini for another cup of tea.

Lini returned to the service area grumbling about the type of people who order tea at a bar as she poured another cup for Emma. It could not have been the quality of the tea that brought this woman back. Lini assumed that Emma was a quasi bag lady who had no better place to go and no better things to do. She returned to Emma's table with teacup in hand and noticed that Emma looked distressed and seemed to be biting down on her finger.

"Are you okay, dear?" Lini asked, trying to be kind.

Emma stammered slightly. It was the nervous, shy stammer of one who really doesn't anticipate anyone caring about anything that matters to her. Emma also tried to manage a smile. Being constructed with the same tools that shaped her psyche, her face was not predisposed to such activity.

"I'm…I'm fine. It's such a beautiful day and well, it's, it's my birth…"

"Hey, sweetie! Get these girls another round. We're parched over here." Marta bellowed her command from across the bar. To Lini, this was not unlike the mooing of some discontented cow from a distant field.

"Be with you in a minute." Lini returned the shout and rolled her eyes at Emma. She gently patted Emma's hand as it lay outstretched upon the table. "We'll talk as soon as I handle the heifers. Sorry, dear." Lini winked and moved to the bar to order four more drinks.

The eyes of the man at the end of the bar followed the scene as it developed before him. He had wandered into this place "in here" to get away from what he perceived to be the hypocrisy of all that existed "out there"—beyond the doors of the bar.

He had just won the Pulitzer Prize. Theoretically, he should feel like he was on top of the world. All of the time he had spent trying to learn to write things meaningful was finally being rewarded, and he just couldn't get his mind around the honor. People who did not like him were singing his praises and offering profuse congratulations. People he neither liked nor respected were pointing to him as a man at the zenith, a man who had reached the pinnacle of a great career.

What should it mean to you when people you don't like love you? What should it mean to you when people who never liked you now honor and pretend to admire you? Obviously, he had experienced a special moment in a lifetime. It was just that the man at the end of the bar thought there would be greater happiness and clarity with the achievement of great success. He had wandered into Sam's Bar, a place he had never been before, to find clarity in anonymity and happiness in the lives of strangers.

This, then, was his one special moment, the time when life and space collide to form a continuum of clarity. He had arrived at the happy place where dreams and reality are as one. He tried to remember the last time he was truly happy. Women he had loved came to mind and evaporated as quickly as they came. He thought that he had found love once or twice, but, at forty, he had come to realize that love didn't really exist. The seemingly random combination of two lives into one was nothing more than that. All else was deconstruction.

The man at the bar searched his mind for a happy time in his past that was so pure and unadulterated that there would be no denying its existence, no explaining it away as something less than a moment of perfection in time.

He remembered a summer's day at a bungalow near his grandmother's house on a bay. He saw himself on the gray wood floor of the green and white house, barefoot because it was incredibly hot that day. His blue shorts matched the blue background of his striped polo shirt and the blue cardboard hat emblazoned with the "stars and bars," which he wore proudly upon his head. The cheap little hat fit him perfectly, and he loved to wear it. The sky was a deep gray, and the heaviness in the air meant a summer thunderstorm was on its way.

The boy had two large soldiers (one blue, one gray)

and two large horses (one blue, one gray). He was playing "Silver War" (it would be years before he learned that the bloodbath was actually a "civil" war). The air was crackling in anticipation of the brewing electrical storm. Still, the boy played on, happy to be imagining what would happen next in the battle of the blue and the gray. He began to move the gray horse forward as a glass filled with whiskey skimmed across the floor, disturbing his concentration and his games of make-believe.

His mother yelled some obscenity at his father which he did not understand. His father said that she was dim-witted and stupid. The tone was as harsh and as severe as the boy had ever heard. The little boy then knew that the Silver War and its reverie would have to wait.

It was time to get out of the way of the storms swirling inside the bungalow and the ugly words that were an intrinsic part of his home. The boy ran down the green stairs that connected the second story of the clapboard house with the wide, sandy path that led to the beach. He was upset, but at least he'd gotten out before things got too rough upstairs.

He jumped off the last step and onto the clover patch of white puffy flowers that he loved to pull from the ground. As he stepped down on his left foot, the boy let out an ungodly scream of pain and anguish; he had landed on a queen bumblebee.

His scream was so loud that it caused the war of the

second story to be suspended for a moment. His parents looked out the window and asked what was wrong, as he sat on the ground, crying. His uncle's fiancée, a woman he'd never liked, cradled him in her arms and offered to remove the stinger from his foot. She had very long nails, an attribute the boy always noticed, which made it easy for her to remove the stinger. She explained what she was doing, and in no time, the boy felt better and ran towards the beach.

Moments later, a cloudburst sent forth a storm, the likes of which he had never seen in his young life. Sheets of cold rain fell from the sky. Trapped between a beach that was becoming quickly flooded and the bungalow filled with the unpredictable violence of his family, he had to make a choice. The boy returned to the bungalow drenched, his favorite hat ruined.

The man seated at the bar shook his head slightly to pull himself back into the reality of his surroundings. So much for the pure and unadulterated happy times of my past, he thought. I guess that's why I became a writer. He turned his attention to the barkeep and requested another beer.

Lini stared at the man from her position in the service area. There was something about him: his detached glance to a vague point in the distance; a sense she had that he was a man comfortable with himself; the fact that he was a good-looking man, obviously involved in the affairs of the world. There was something drawing her to him. She had never felt this way about any of the patrons of Sam's Bar before, but she knew she had to do something about this feeling. She had to meet him, but she didn't know how to approach him. She decided to position herself so that she might accidentally fall within his field of vision.

The man at the bar drank another deep draught of the beer before him. His thoughts returned to the Pulitzer. It had just happened yesterday. This was his moment. "Greatest Newspaperman in the World...Advanced Society...Made people listen who didn't want to hear... The entire world sat up and took notice..." The man harrumphed into his beer and ran his fingers through his thinning hair. "Top of the world? In a pig's eye." He knew that he should have felt more attachment to this honor, but he was having trouble ginning up any enthusiasm for the prize.

He looked at the paper that led with his story. Because of the Pulitzer, it was reprinted "above the fold" again. "Below the fold" sat facing him on the bar. He flipped the paper over to see his lead. "The story that made the world sit up and take notice" was soaking up stale beer from the scratched and pitted bar.

Alcohol soaked through every memory he ever had. As a child, he lived with this pollutant that made the waters of his life a sea that "good people" always tried to avoid. As an adult, he picked up a glass for a number of reasons—mostly, to forget, sometimes, to help reconcile himself to the superfluous smiles of a world for which he had little use. The man at the bar was having a hard time mustering up a smile today.

Somehow he had managed to win the prize. He wondered what others might say about him if they knew. There had been so many who had been so important at so many different times in his life. Jeannie would have known it was important, though perhaps not why. Kipla would have seen its potential influence on his career and impact on his finances. Toni would have wished that she knew more about it, so she could feel what it was that he felt. Then there was Robi; what would Robi say?

His thoughts were interrupted by a loud belch, followed by inebriated laughter.

"You sound like my first husband, Marta," laughed one of the women. She wiped her mouth and nose with one swipe of her hand and snorted slightly as she laughed.

The man at the bar noticed that the woman named Marta wore gold knit shoes. The fat from her toes seemed to be crammed back into the borders of her shoes, creating quarter-inch-thick pillows of fat where the gold knit met the flesh.

He looked at the feet of the other women at the table and noticed fat curling over the edges of every shoe that he could see. He wondered how comfortable they could be. He wondered if their feet retained their odd appearance even after they took off their shoes.

Again, the stranger shook his head slightly to move from these thoughts and this reality to something a bit more interesting and compatible with his general disposition. He noticed the waitress was now standing before him, her serving tray clutched tightly to her chest, wearing a sweet smile that could convey nothing other than an overture of friendship.

Eyes glistening with a smile that would not quit, she extended her hand to him.

"My name is Lini. I couldn't help but notice you when you came in. I know that this might seem a bit strange and forward, but I really did want to make your acquaintance."

The man smiled slightly, nodded his head, tipped his glass of beer, and said, "Acquaintance made."

Lini felt like an absolute fool. If she could have comfortably crawled away from that spot, she would have done so. She felt like everyone in the bar was laughing at her as she stood there feeling her cheeks redden and her spirits sink. She let the tray fall to her sides as she tried to express herself with more humor and personality.

"Well, yes, great. You know I just wanted to say hello. We don't often get men like you in here, and I just wanted to say hello." This was going nowhere. Lini had just said hello twice to emphasize that she wanted to say hello.

Looking around the bar, the man smiled at her again.

"Doesn't look like you get many men in here at all."

"Oh. Yeah. Well, this is a little unusual for us. But I don't know…now that you mention it, maybe not." Lini was horrified by the fact that she had never noticed how few men came into this bar. No wonder she never met anyone.

Lini faded into her calculations of how many men had ever come into Sam's. The man at the bar was becoming visibly uncomfortable as he considered the silent woman before him. He wondered if this was going to be another of those "empty escalator" relationships he had experienced so often in his life. He had grown tired of the seemingly endless series of steps in relationships that always appeared to be different and moving but all ended in the very same place, having gone nowhere at all. Still, this woman was beautiful, and he sensed that she had endearing qualities that might be worth the effort. She seemed funny in an odd sort of way. He asked her to sit beside him.

Lini was shaken out of her reverie. "Me? Sit down? Oh yeah…sure. Well, actually, no. I'm working, you see."

The bartender, who had spent years watching the melodrama that was Lini, saw an opportunity to do a good deed. "Take a break, Lini. I think I can handle this huge crowd."

Lini smiled at Mac, and he returned the favor. Lini sat beside the man whom she wanted to meet. As he walked away, Mac heard the man introduce himself as Jim Dooley.

The writer? Mac wondered. Lini might have stumbled onto the jackpot this time. The bartender stood by the drink garnishes and heard Dooley ask Lini something about Santa Claus. The bartender smiled to himself.

As he washed glasses, he thought about Lini. He had known Lini for two years, and he had never known her to be truly happy. She had dated a number of guys Mac would describe as "bar losers"—funny and abusive, rich and abusive, or cute and abusive. The abuse was mostly mental, but Mac remembered one guy who, he thought, was a little too rough with Lini.

She mucked her way through life and its relationships but never really seemed to be getting anywhere. She always wanted a guy to be there, no matter what his quality. Mac looked back at Lini and Dooley. They were laughing, and she was touching his arm as she spoke to him. Lini seemed to be enjoying herself, and Mac felt good for her. He washed the glasses with a little more enthusiasm than usual.

Suddenly, a woman yelled for more drinks. Lini stopped her conversation, looked at the woman, and then looked at the bartender. He held up his hand to assure her that there was nothing to worry about. He served the woman more drinks—and Emma more tea—without breaking a sweat.

Returning to the bar, he began to think about Lini some more. She had always told him that there was not a man in the world worth calling in sick for; the job—and the money and security it provided—was necessary for when the man decided to leave. Only someone hopelessly, helplessly, and "happily ever after" in love could afford that luxury. The bartender sadly shook his head; Lini had never missed a day.

Emma sat in the corner. Tears were welling up in her eyes again. Hadn't Lini told her that she would be coming back to speak with her? What was she doing fawning over that man at the bar?

This was always the case with Emma. In high school, and again in college, whenever she went out with her girlfriends, Emma was always the one left behind when her friends paired up with the boys they met. She always had to find her own way home—alone. Years ago, she stopped going out with others—it hurt too much. Being lonely never felt too great, either. Still, it hurt less to be alone than to be left alone, so she always kept people away. She had no family, and no one knew where she lived. No one knew she had six cats and three dogs. The animals were her family. They were all she could rely upon. They were always happy to see her. This almost made her smile.

"Last call!" Mac announced.

"Double down, brother," cried an inebriated Marta. Her friends laughed. The bartender complied and brought two more drinks for all the women at the table. Emma, not wanting to be last, abruptly stood up and left the bar.

Dooley and Lini continued their conversation, laughing, comfortable in each other's company, and oblivious to their surroundings.

"That was some break," Dooley said, as his eyes, still moist with laughter, looked steadily into Lini's. "How does this place make any money?"

"I'm independently wealthy, can't you tell?" Mac smiled and winked at Lini. "I don't need this place at all."

Lini's head tilted slightly as she smiled at the bartender and reached out to grasp his hand. "Thanks so much, Mac. I owe you big time."

"You owe me nothing, Lini. Now, you two get out of here before I lose my license for serving after hours." The couple got up and turned to leave. Mac thought that his little joke about them leaving together would get them to stay together for tonight, maybe longer. Like most bartenders, a drunken romantic lurked somewhere close to the cynical surface of his being. He smiled to himself. He felt that he had done a number of good deeds for the day, and he was proud. He turned off the light behind the bar and herded the table of suburban women to their car.

At about ten-thirty the next morning, the phone on the bar rang. Mac had been cleaning rocks glasses, and a towel was draped over his shoulder. For some reason, he felt particularly optimistic that morning. Maybe it was a feeling carried over from the night before; it felt good to see Lini so happy. She was a great kid, and he looked at her more as his little sister than as an employee. The phone rang again.

"I'm comin', I'm comin'...geez Louise." He slammed his hand on the bottom of the receiver and caught the phone in mid air. "Yellow?" he said.

"Hel-loooo," a loud and very happy voice called across the line. "Mac, my love, is that you?"

"No, it's Clark Gable. What in the world of sports do you want? Where are you?"

"That, my dear, is classified. How are *you* today?" The caller laughed coquettishly.

"Don't act like you care. What do you want?"

The voice laughed excitedly into the phone. "Guess what? I am calling in *sick* today."

"Are you ill? I mean, other than mentally?"

"I am in love," the voice replied in a throaty and theatrical whisper.

Not wanting to get caught up in Lini's cosmic reverie, Mac replied: "Don't fall too hard or too fast, sister. Sometimes things are not exactly as they seem. Sometimes people are only sixty or seventy percent of what you need, and you think that they're the whole package. Give it time. There may be greater fish in the sea that look and sound just like this guy and are better suited for you and your particular brand of insanity."

"Fish, schmish, what do you know about love, you dried-up old mutt? This is the real thing. The connections are sooooo strong. We spent the entire night talking, laughing, and sharing the history of our lives. This is the *real thing*. This feeling can never end. Guess where we went this morning."

Mac smiled slightly, "I must admit that I am beyond guessing where you two went this morning."

"We went to the old Clayborne cemetery! He loves old cemeteries as much as I do. We stood looking at the headstones, constructing stories from the writing on the stones. It was amazing! We also saw this mystical cat that appeared like a witch out of nowhere. Dooley says it just wandered into the cemetery from Lakehorne Road, but I swear this thing just appeared out of thin air, just like a witch."

"Well, my dear, that is why people sleep at night—so they don't see witch cats appearing in old cemeteries on dew-soaked mornings like this. Please take the day off. It sounds like you'd be no good to me here, anyway. Have fun. But remember what I said about too far, too fast."

"Yes… Yes, whatever, Daddy dearest. Thanks a lot. I'll see you tomorrow."

Lini hung up and Mac slowly returned the receiver to its cradle. He thought about Lini's schoolgirl enthusiasm and hoped, for her sake, that this would be the real thing—whatever that was. Maybe, finally, Lini had gotten lucky.

He stopped for a moment to think about his own life and the women he had loved and lost. Thoughts about his past brought few smiles to his face. His memory was inadequate when it came to reconstructing faces and places. Maybe he'd spent too many nights drinking in small, smoky bars. Maybe he'd never pulled anyone too close to him. Maybe he wasn't as lucky as Lini appeared to be. Maybe he never really tried hard enough to find The One. He had been married twice, but those situations seemed to lose their sense of reality and importance rather quickly. He had had his share of good times in his life, of that he was sure, but he felt them to be insignificant—too insignificant to speak about. But then, he thought that maybe life was just a series of insignificant events. Even the most significant events are insignificant to someone. So maybe all life was just a waste of time! His gaze was lost in the rocks glasses.

"Is Lini here?" Emma asked, as Mac almost did a triple axel out of his socks.

"Jesus Christ almighty, Emma! I wish that you wouldn't do that. We're not open yet. What are you doing here?"

Emma was taken aback. "The door was open. I just thought I could come in. I was looking for Lini. Is she here? She told me yesterday that she was going to speak with me and she never did. Do you know where she is?"

The lines in Mac's face pulled together in a pattern of disbelief. "Lini was supposed to speak with you?! When? Yesterday, last night, this morning? What in the hell are you talking about, Emma?"

Emma began to retreat into the shell of shyness from which she had been functioning for the past forty years. She was easily intimidated and it showed. She stammered slightly as she responded to Mac. She was annoyed and ashamed that Mac found it so unusual that Lini would want to speak with her. She looked briefly at the bar and then beyond Mac's face. "It… It… It was before closing, before she met *that man*," she responded, emphasizing the noun too much for Mac's taste. "She went to get me some tea, tapped my hand, and said she'd get back to speak with me, but she never did. Where is she? I need to speak with her."

Mac slammed the bar with his hand, and it was Emma's turn to jump.

"Whoa," he said, scratching his broad stomach in an unconscious manner that showed his lack of respect for Emma.

"Let me get this straight…Lini says, 'I'll be back, we'll talk' in the middle of a busy shift, and you take that as meaning that you two have a date to converse? What are you —nuts?! Get outta here. Come back when we're open. Lini won't be here, though; she's out with *that man*," Mac concluded, with mock emphasis on his last two words.

Emma felt betrayed as she made her way towards the door. She muttered something to herself about men and walked out.

"Nuts," Mac muttered to himself as he waved Emma out of the bar. He'd seen too many in his lifetime, and they always annoyed him—probably more than they should. Lini had started his day well, and now he was convinced that this was going to be one of those days, thanks to his visit from the Mistress of Twisted Strawberries, a pet name that he had developed for Emma a long time ago.

Dooley and Lini spent the day doing the things that lovers do early in a relationship to see whether there is a special bond between them. They were trying to find out how much they could enjoy each other's company.

They sat on bright white Adirondack chairs perched on a bluff overlooking the ocean. They seemed to be placed there because of the magnificent view, but Lini and Dooley were using them as vehicles of insight into each other's hearts. They spoke of their personal histories and made childish jokes. Each dared the other to jump into the cool surf of spring without the benefit of clothing. Could each person be as wild as the other's fantasy would allow?

They didn't know who owned the chairs or the stairs that led from the bluff to the ocean's edge. Lini and Dooley had stolen them in the name of love and intimacy; they would never surrender their memory to any mortal unfamiliar with the everlasting beauty of unselfish love. An odd person interrupted their reverie, asking for directions in this directionless place. The juxtaposition and imposition of reality into their talk of dreams and fantasy made them laugh. The world was interfering again.

The world was a funny place that was a canvas for their love and humor. The world was the one thing they had in common. They spoke about how ridiculous it may have seemed, but as they searched and learned more about each other, they discovered that their minds so closely overlapped and saw things in much the same way, that the world was always "out there" and only Lini and Dooley existed "in here." Where "there" and "here" were would always be a subject for discussion, but Lini felt "here" was her heart and soul. She decided that she wasn't going to listen to Mac at all. Lini's heart, soul, and mind were given freely to Jim Dooley without a second thought about the consequences.

The first day after the first night, it was as if God himself were confirming that two great forces in his creation had finally found each other again. No one ever speaks of Edenic love, as a way of describing the love that Adam and Eve must have had for each other. No one speaks of a love between two beautiful beings in a most perfect place created for each other as a symbol for all love and nature. This was the love that Lini felt for Dooley, the unquestioning love of another that doesn't allow the morals and values of a civilization's lineage to interfere with its simple, elegant beauty. Lini would later say that she finally understood what all those songwriters and poets were feeling when they wrote pieces that she always found so sappy. Still, she felt that her feelings were far deeper and more profound than those. When one believes she has found perfect love, she doesn't believe that "more perfect" exists.

The day after the first night, God created a huge thunderstorm, with hailstones falling from the heavens, and a downpour that would have made a modern-day Noah consider the construction of an ark. Abandoning their chairs atop the ocean's bluff, Lini and Dooley made their way to a small coffee shop; there, they watched the weather of the real world from a few wooden stools, leaning over a table topped in Formica, learning more about each other's heart and soul.

When the storm passed, and the short-term flooding of the streets had subsided, Lini and Dooley left the coffee shop to survey the damage. A beautiful rainbow seemed to span the cape by the ocean's edge in the little harbor town.

Lini spoke about the Biblical nature of the weather and how it must mean something; this kind of weather just didn't happen every day. Dooley looked at her and smiled thinly, keeping his thoughts private for the moment. The sun was setting, dusk was upon them, and without knowing why, he reached to put his arms around Lini.

"With all my mind, with all my heart, with all my soul, Lini," he said as he hugged her. She knew what he meant and a feeling developed within her, a feeling she had never experienced before.

She asked Dooley to hold her again. An almost imperceptible sway began to develop as they held each other. The love they had found caused them such joy that they danced unconsciously in each other's arms.

Lini asked Dooley to take her home. They had an evening of lovemaking that was beyond anything either of them had ever experienced in their lives. The intensity of the feeling was so great that it was not just the feeling of two bodies linked in time, but two bodies that became two souls embracing each other, passing through each other, using every nuance of physicality and language to express undying adoration of each other.

They would talk about love and the intensity of feeling while making love, and they would talk about life and everything that influenced them when they were not making love.

Dooley spoke of his family and his dysfunctional past that led him to want to be so much more in life. Lini told him that her family had been too good, too supportive, sometimes making her feel that she could never be that good; and yet, she could never fail because her family would always love her.

The night and the day and the night ended with much love, much sharing, and not much sleep. Dooley was on a Pulitzer hiatus, but Lini knew that she had to get back to work at the bar. She couldn't call in sick another day.

They walked into Mac's empty bar arm in arm with broad smiles upon their faces. They had just seen something on the street that struck them as funny, yet they knew that there was no sense in describing this incident of shared humor to Mac. Even Mac would have a way of being a real-world intruder in their Eden.

Eying the smiling couple, Mac asked, "Had an awful day off, Lini? Happy to be back at work? Strap on an apron and let's get ready for our booming evening business."

Of course, Lini had no time for the cynical, rhetorical question posed by Mac. She just began the prep work as she always did. Mac shook Dooley's hand, and they shared a laugh and a beer as Lini went about her work. For the next few days, Lini, Mac, and Dooley fell into a wonderful routine of love, fun, and laughter.

It had been a week since Lini and Dooley had started seeing each other when Emma finally returned to the bar. She sat alone in the corner as she always did. Lini said a heartfelt and happy hello. As usual, something was bothering Emma, but she wouldn't say what it was. Lini tried to speak with her a few times, but Emma would have nothing of it. Her sullen disposition seemed to grow deeper with every laugh that Mac, Lini, and Dooley shared. Emma drank her tea and watched sports that she didn't understand on the television.

The suburban hausfraus arrived early and drank hard. Dooley now felt comfortable enough with Mac to share his impressions and insights regarding their demeanor and appearance. The two men shared large laughs.

Yet for all the laughs, jokes, and pleasant atmosphere that had grown so refreshingly comfortable to Dooley, there was not a night, not a moment, when his eyes left Lini. There were times he would sit back in his chair and admire what, to him, was an absolute beauty. The way she bit the side of her lip or tossed her hair were, to him, exquisite. He loved everything about her. There were times when he wished that he could program his brain to permanently remember how beautiful she was in a particular situation.

On this particular night, Dooley asked Mac if he could let Lini off a little early. He wanted to plan a special trip for them, and he was excited about speaking to Lini about his plans. In spite of Mac's fear that he would soon lose a good waitress, he told Lini that she could knock off early and that he would clean up.

Lini wanted to know what all the mystery was about, but she welcomed more time with Dooley. Emma had just left her place in the bar muttering to herself. Lini cleared her table.

Marta and her friends, more inebriated than ever, looked like they were winding down and getting ready to leave. Lini didn't feel guilty about the fact that she might be leaving Mac too much work to do.

It was a crisp, cool, beautiful evening for a walk. The warm winds of late March and early April had not yet arrived. The air seemed more like late October, frosted by the occasional wisps of vapor emanating from the mouths of Lini and Dooley as they continued their stimulating conversations about nothing.

Lini had grown to notice something about Dooley. Whenever he had something important to say, he would minimize it with some silly introduction. When he wanted to say something odd or silly, he would always lead with a ponderous statement or question. This evening he was being excessively silly, so she knew that something important was on his mind. Dovetailing his actions with the fact that they had left the bar early, Lini wondered where all this would lead.

Dooley was making Lini laugh with some story about Mac doing an Irish jig when they noticed Emma, across the street, looking grave and distraught.

Dooley called out. "Emma, are you okay? Emma, look! Saint Patrick's Day is coming." Dooley performed a silly jig. Emma's head barely moved; apart from that, she did not react at all.

Lini gave an exaggerated wave to which Emma did not respond.

Lini called out, in her best English accent, "Emma, come. We'll share tea together." Still, there was no reply.

Lini looked at Dooley, and they shrugged shoulders simultaneously. They were about to move on when they decided to take one last shot at rousting Emma. Dooley danced and waved again. This time, Emma stared right at them.

She looked across the street at the foolish man who had caused all of the unsettling changes in her life, and decided that her decision was final. She would not be left behind again. She would not be alone again. She'd show them. Emma stepped off the curb and in front of a car that was speeding toward the corner.

Dooley shouted and instinctively ran towards her. The speeding BMW braked hard, swerved, and knocked Dooley into the air. His body landed on the roof of the car. Lini screamed. Emma jumped back, fell on the curb, and started to cry.

Marta yelled from the car, "What in the hell was that?"

Lini ran toward Dooley. He rolled off the top of the car, glancing off her arms as he fell back onto the street. He was unconscious, but his heart was beating. One of the women in the car called the police.

Emma sat on the curb with her head in her hands. She was unhurt.

The next thing she knew, Lini was sitting in the ambulance with Dooley, crying as they raced towards the hospital. Dooley was recognized by a member of the hospital staff as they wheeled him into the emergency room. Regaining some measure of lucidity, Dooley confirmed his identity to the team that was treating him. Due to the severity of the accident and the uncertainty of Dooley's condition, his sister, as next of kin, was contacted.

Lini phoned Mac and told him that there had been an accident. "I am at the hospital now, Mac. It looks bad."

As Lini briefed him on what had happened, Mac scrubbed his face and thought about all that could go wrong. He knew that Lini would need someone to be with her. "I'll lock up and come right over. I'll be there as soon as I can."

Mac told the few customers in the bar that there was an emergency and that he would have to close up. He locked the door and ran to his car. As he drove, he cursed the luck that would allow this to happen. He was worried about Lini. She would not be strong enough to handle any great tragedy very well. She'd be crushed if anything ever happened to Dooley. Mac parked his car and ran to the emergency room. He embraced a red-eyed Lini, who burst into tears when she saw him. Lini stood in the emergency room crying on Mac's shoulder, unable to control herself.

Soon, Dooley's sister, her assistant, and the family

chauffeur strode into the hospital. Angrily, she demanded that she meet the doctor in charge of her brother's care.

Mac, seeing things a little more clearly through his misted eyes, nodded slightly and reached down to hold Lini's hand.

After about twenty minutes, a doctor came into the waiting room to speak with Lini. She stood quivering with anticipation, Mac's arm around her shoulder.

The doctor spoke first, "He's all right. Physically, he's okay."

Lini interrupted, "Can I see him?"

The doctor was visibly uncomfortable and stern. "Well, no, not yet... He's experiencing a sort of traumatic amnesia. I've informed his sister of the situation, and she is with him now. Since you brought him here and seem to have some sort of relationship to him, I have obtained her permission to tell you about his condition."

"You mean he doesn't know who he is?" Lini asked, horrified.

"No, no. This isn't TV. Mr. Dooley knows who he is. He knows where he's been. It's just that his short-term memory has suffered a trauma. He'll be fine, but it's possible that there might be a few black holes in his memory."

"Well, can I see him?" Lini started to cry again. She was worried about the black holes.

The doctor looked down at the black linoleum tile floor and shuffled his feet slightly. "That's really up to the next of kin; Mr. Dooley's sister has just recently arrived. I will tell you this: We had him up briefly to see if he could recognize you and your friend here. He had no idea who you were. I'll send the sister out in a few minutes. You can talk to her about the situation. I'm sorry." The doctor walked away with his head slightly bowed, rubbing his chin.

Lini was now sobbing uncontrollably. She was sitting back in her chair, shocked and saddened beyond words. Mac moved to comfort her, but he had no idea what he should say. There was no way he could be prepared for this. How could he help Lini cope with the situation?

After a few minutes that seemed like a lifetime to Lini, Dooley's sister approached Lini and Mac. Where Dooley was warm and open, his sister struck them as cold. Where Dooley always seemed like a man who cared little for the trappings of his station in life, it seemed that his sister, with the mink coat and the chauffeur, was one of those people who used material privilege to justify her existence.

In a rather removed way, Dooley's sister extended her hand to Lini. "I understand that you brought my brother here this evening. Thank you. You are very kind."

Lini, now suffering in five different ways at once, was certain that if she didn't say something fast, this woman was going to walk away. Lini didn't know what to say, and suddenly she just blurted out, "We are in love, you know."

The look of condescension that overcame the face of Dooley's sister was quite pronounced. Her words dripped with derision. "Oh, really? You and my brother are in love? Funny, I've never seen you before. And my brother doesn't even know your name."

"My name is Lini. And, well, we've not said it, but we've certainly felt the love between us. We've been dating this past week. We've spent all of our free time together."

Mac chimed in. "I can vouch for that."

"Oh, you can, now? Well, isn't that nice. Listen, a week of sexcapades with my dear brother does not qualify as love. If that were true, he'd have been in love dozens of times in the last few years alone!" The sister was regaining her composure and the cool, confident elitism that she wore so comfortably. "Thank you for helping him. I'll be sure that you get some sort of reward. Leave your name and address with my chauffeur. If Dooley ever does ask for you, we'll be sure to give you a call." She turned and walked away.

Lini stood frozen in time. Tears returned to her eyes. She could not speak. Finally, she spoke the only syllable that her mouth could form. "Mac… Mac…" Mac moved towards her and wrapped his arms around Lini to console her. He patted her back gently and said that it would all be okay. He didn't believe a word he was saying. Tears began to form in his eyes.

Lini broke free of Mac's grasp and ran towards the room that Dooley's sister had entered. Two men moved in front of the door and told her that they were under orders not to allow her in.

Lini ran back to Mac. Her life was crumbling around her, and she had no idea of how she could stop it. Mac put his arms around her again. "Let's go home, darlin'. We'll find a way to get in touch with Dooley again."

They walked toward Mac's car slowly. Lini cried every step of the way. The streets that had brought her such joy, the places that had brought her such laughter, seemed empty and lacking now. She felt as alone as she had ever felt in her entire life. She felt as though there were ghosts in every brick, every tree, every shrub of the town whose existence she'd never witness again though they'd be with her every day—reminding her by their absence of what was not there. Where before, she and Dooley had stood outside of man's creation and reality, close to Eden together as happy observers of all, she now just stood outside of everything—alone. As she walked with Mac, she noticed that, for the first time in what had seemed like a very long time, she heard her footfalls as she walked down the street. She didn't think that she could ever be happy in that town again.

For a time, she continued to look for Dooley, trying to approach him again and again. She was constantly rebuffed by his family and what Lini imagined to be a newfound relationship with his sister. As time went on, she tried to forget him. It was as if she were trying to forget her own name. To forget Dooley was to deny the existence of the very best parts of her being, the parts that she gave to him which he had already forgotten. Trying to find a different way to forget him, Lini tried to hate him. Lini imagined that Dooley was living a perfectly happy life somewhere without a moment's thought about her.

As for Emma, she was even a failure in her attempt to commit suicide. When she saw the damage her actions had caused, she went home and never returned to Sam's Bar again. Months after the accident, the local newspapers ran a story about a recluse whose apartment windows had been left open through the spring and summer. Someone finally decided that this was unusual and pushed in the door of the apartment. A badly decomposed and partially eaten body was found on the floor. Various dead animal carcasses were found in other rooms of the apartment. Apparently, all had been dead for some time. The human victim was dressed in what appeared to be a cream-colored dress covered with vines and strawberries.

As for Lini, she continued to function. Her face was creased with lines of care and experience. She laughed less easily than she used to. She continued to serve the hausfraus endless rounds of boilermakers while they laughed at their profoundly idiotic conversations.

"Only the stupid survive, kid," Mac would say, as he

rolled his eyes and smiled thinly at Lini, saddened and bitter on her behalf.

One evening, as Lini waited for Mac to pour the drinks for Marta and her girlfriends, an attractive man at the bar looked at her and smiled. Lini returned an autopilot smile.

"Excuse me," he began. "I have a question for you. Do you have a minute?"

"Sure," said Lini, impatiently. "What?"

"Well, why in the world did we create Santa Claus? Why do we set up every Christian kid to believe in a kind, happy soul who shares his love with all once a year, knowing full well that he never has and never will exist? Why do we set children up for certain, crushing disappointment?"

He smiled at Lini and eagerly awaited her response. Lini stared at the man for a second, briefly considered what she just heard, and looked at Mac as he brought her another round of drinks.

"You know what, Mac? You're right...only the stupid survive." She beckoned to the man at the bar. "Here, come with me. I've got a table of suburban hotties for you who are just dying to answer your questions."

The man looked at Mac, looked at Lini, and then shrugged his shoulders and walked out of the bar.

Lost Sailor

Four o'clock was "happy hour" in Lucky Jake's. Barmaids with strategically placed shamrocks and wishbones tucked into their garters hustled around the bar distributing twenty-five cent drinks to the already inebriated horde. The bar was a mob scene. Dollar bills clenched tightly in determined fists were being thrust over equally determined shoulders and heads as drinks of all varieties were shouted to the discriminating ears of the bartenders. Refugees starving for a draught jockeyed for position. Everyone in the bar had come to drink. Everyone wanted to get drunk. A small, yet boisterous, herd disturbed Link's concentration as he sat at the bar.

Link had not come to Lucky Jake's for the happy hour; he had been swept up in it. He drank at Lucky Jake's every day. All the employees knew him. Some of them treated him with pity, which annoyed him, but most were genuinely concerned about him. Link felt comfortable in Lucky Jake's. He would stare at his drink (usually beer), or at a distant candle on the other side of the room, caught up in thoughts about days gone by. Sometimes he would talk to the bartenders or one of the girls, but most of the time he was consumed by his thoughts.

The boisterous group at the bar had disturbed him because they were trying to deface Lucky Jake's. One of them had attempted to carve his initials on the wall with a knife. The bouncers took his knife away and threw him out. A small scuffle had ensued. Link caught the eye of his favorite bartender and shook his head in disgust. The bartender brought him a fresh, cold beer to relieve the tension.

"Take it easy, Link. Just another asshole from some goddamn place. He can't understand that this place belongs to someone else. He don't know shit, Link. Drink up and cool off—it's on me, buddy." He smiled and slapped Link's shoulder.

A drunken junior executive turned to Link and smiled stupidly. "Hey, man, they know you here. You get damn good service." He held out his hand and grinned rather foolishly. "My name is Layne Kirkland. I sell business equipment. It's a little loud in here—I didn't get your name."

For a moment, Link examined the paw extended before him. In the unusual light of Lucky Jake's, it looked sweaty, green, and without callus. In an act of penance, he shook the body part and introduced himself without interest or enthusiasm. The executive was bubbling like cheap champagne, as he rambled on about the difficulties of his job. Link nodded appropriately at all hesitations and smiled at every joke.

Link's mind had started to drift as he nodded at another particularly inane comment made by the junior executive, when his nose picked up a friendly and familiar scent. It was Mary's perfume. She never changed it. Link looked to his right and saw the shamrocks and wishbone tucked into the garter that stretched around his favorite thigh.

Mary was a long-legged blonde who saved her sweetest smiles for Link. She would embrace him and kiss his cheek whenever she saw him. She had been a barmaid at Lucky Jake's for a few years and probably knew Link as well as anyone, although she felt that she didn't know him at all. They'd had many long talks together. Lately, she had become worried about Link because his talks had changed. He no longer discussed the things that used to concern him. His conversation had become more superficial and trivial. There was no longer great fire and light raging behind his steel blue eyes—his mind had become a cavern that only the most skillful spelunker could navigate. He would shrug his shoulders rather than open his mouth.

Mary wondered about what had been troubling Link lately. She felt that she was losing touch with the one open nerve she had found in her body of friends. Link's mind was scabbing over and becoming secretive. Was it her? Or was he becoming one of "them"? She couldn't bear to see the man she loved transform himself into a hollow shell waltzing through life rather than a whip striking out at a target. She tried to get closer and closer to him as he withdrew further and further into himself. She was terrified that her lack of knowledge would drive him to some dark dead end from which there was no escape.

Mary's intuition told her that Link was "back at that place" again. "It's a hard place to imagine unless you've lived through it yourself," Link used to say. "Once you've lived there, you never want to go back, but you never really leave, so you can't help but go back. Each time you get there, you think you can change the outcome, or the relevance, or the situation, or the decision, but you can't. All those things have already happened, and yet, it's like seeing the same two roads fork before you every day; you always take the right road because that's the road you know—making that decision never puts you in any different place. You live out the day and find yourself back at the same fork with the same decision before you and the same plan in your head." Link always told her that this wasn't a place for spring flowers and park benches; it wasn't a place for yellow curtains and chocolate cakes. It was so hard to describe because it is such a hard place to live.

"Satisfaction and frustration are trees that share the

same root," he'd say, and then, inevitably, he'd smile and wink at Mary and assure her that "he was just babbling again" and that he'd get over it. There would always be some period of time when she thought he really was "over it." Then he would get real silent or talk in twisted riddles, and Mary knew he was "back at that place again" and that there was nothing she could do to get him out of it. He always needed time. Mary wondered if Link was beginning to realize that time might be the one thing he was running out of.

Putting all visible clues of her cares and misgivings about him aside, Mary smiled at Link as he turned to her and then she kissed him. She gave him a look of mock surprise when he introduced her to Layne Kirkland. She then gave Mr. Kirkland a look of absolute disgust as he surveyed her form from head to toe. Link was very drunk now. The bartenders had taken good care of him. Mary mentioned the fact that he was a little less than sober as he put his arm around her waist.

"You shoulda seen it, Miss," Kirkland slurred. "I've never seen such service in my life. This bar was packed as it could be, but my friend here kept getting us drinks whenever we wanted 'em. Damndest thing I ever saw. I asked him his secret. You know what he said? You gotta take care of the bartenders—tip 'em real good. Yup. Only, I didn't see this old scoundrel lay one nickel down on the bar." He slapped Link's arm.

For a moment, the fire returned to Link's eyes. He stared at the inattentive and inebriated Mr. Kirkland. "Old scoundrel indeed. Me—a scoundrel? Can you believe that, Mary? Why, I could tell stories that would make this pup squirm in his seat."

Mary looked at Link with concern.

Link straightened himself up in his chair. Happy hour was over, and he could speak in softer tones now. "I will tell this one all about me, how I got here, and what happened." He rubbed his nose and swayed slightly in his seat as he spoke. "Yeah…I should tell him that story." He seemed to lose consciousness as he sat there thinking about his past.

An invisible slap from an unknown hand seemed to rouse Link to great enthusiasm. He began to speak. "Kirkland, my boy, you need to hear this one…"

At that moment, his afternoon of drinking caught up with Link, and before he could speak another word, his face fell into the beer mug before him. Kirkland chuckled slightly as Mary cleaned Link up and tried to move him. One of the bouncers carried him to a room in the back.

Kirkland looked Mary over again and smiled drunkenly. "How about leaving that old souse and coming over to my place?"

Mary slapped a five dollar bill on the bar. "There's your cab fare, boy. Get your ass home and out of my sight." Mary left for the back room to find Link.

One of the bartenders approached Kirkland. "You'll never score with her. She loves that guy. She'd do anything for him."

Kirkland couldn't believe it. As his elbow slipped off the bar, he exclaimed, "She loves that ragged old drunk? Man, he looks like the type of guy who sleeps in the subway."

It was the bartender's turn to become annoyed.

"Don't ever say shit like that about Link. He's a good man. I know. You want to hear a story? I'll tell you about him."

He placed another beer in front of Kirkland.

"Link used to be a fine young executive, a real prospect. He had brains. He had common sense. He had an idea on how to handle the endless corporate bullshit that guys like you put up with every day. Link had money then—lots of money. He worked all the time and had no time to spend his earnings. He would stop in here once, maybe twice a week, buy a few beers, talk to Mary, and leave.

"One day, he told us about a great deal he was working on. He was going to invest everything he had in a giant parcel of land out west. This guy he was working with knew the land—he was sure there was oil. Link threw all of his money in, and his friend began poking holes in the ground. Damned if they didn't strike oil—lots of it. Link's friend came back to get him to move out west to administrate the business. This guy drove up to our door in the biggest damn limousine you ever saw. He came walking into this place in a damn tuxedo. I was impressed. I mean this guy was nothing more than a damn hole puncher, and he was dressed to kill. Link was sitting down here in his usual seat, sipping his beer.

"The guy in the tuxedo asks for Link like he's never seen him before. He acted like he was too important to look for Link himself. Anyway, I turn to point Link out to this dude, and Link is gone. I told him that Link must have gone out the back door and maybe he'd catch him if he hurried.

"The man grimaced like he was really being put out and went out the door to find Link. I don't know, but if you asked me at the time, it didn't seem like 'tuxedo man' was moving at top speed. Anyway, I have to piece the rest of this together from what Mary has told me—and she ain't too free to talk about Link.

"She was coming into work as this guy was leaving. She saw Link in the alley looking like he was trying to hide from something or get away from somebody. He waved to her, motioned for silence, grabbed her elbow, and walked away from the man in the tuxedo like he was death in the flesh. The man called to them, asking if they knew Link. Link muttered 'No!' and Mary shouted it back to the man. The exasperated man in the tuxedo then ended his search for the friend who had put him there and sped off in his limousine.

"Mary looked at Link and asked him if he was in any kind of trouble. Link smiled at her and said the damnedest thing—'Not anymore.' Mary didn't understand. She asked him about time spent, energy used, money gone and wasted. Link paused in the middle of the street and stared at her for a few moments before he said anything. Then, he smiled. 'At least I won't die administering holes in the ground, counting my money, and forgetting my friends.' Mary thought he had lost it, but he said he never felt better. He felt he had done something with his life.

"As Mary looked at his face, she said you could see a subtle transformation take place. The creases at the edges of his eyes seemed to soften slightly, a wry smile appeared, and his eyes brightened and widened as he struggled for the words to say.

"Finally, with a broader smile and a wilder look in his eyes, he told Mary that he couldn't write poetry, but he had just decided he'd do his damnedest to live it. She then said something to Link that he sometimes mentions today—I think it really haunts him. Anyway, she told Link that livin' poetry is real neat, but it doesn't matter if no one reads it.

"She knew that she was looking at the electric excitement in Link's eyes with a certain sadness in her own.

Her Irish mother used to say, 'People die and their grave-stones erode at equal rates, but people who leave something behind live just a tiny bit longer.' Mary had always lived her life that way: She had no concept of living in the minute or the moment; she lived to live longer.

"She wished she could have been able to share in what was to Link a huge victory. She wished that she could have been more supportive. She wished that for that day, at that moment, she could have forgotten the stern words of her Irish ma. But she always says that she'll never forget the tinge of sadness and the short droop of disappointment that took over Link's face for just a moment before he regained control of his features and forced her to join in his euphoric state.

"Link told her that he didn't want to live any longer than he had to. He only wanted the poetry to live behind him. She didn't have the heart to tell him, but she told me, that she doesn't think the poetry exists. Goddamn, isn't that wild? Hey…Kirkland. Wake up man!"

Kirkland had fallen asleep during the bartender's story. His face lay in a puddle of warm beer on the bar.

As the story ended, Link and Mary came out of the back room. Link looked to be fully recovered. He smiled and waved to the bartender and laughed at Kirkland when he saw him asleep.

"Boring the customers again, Joe? Man, I've got to think up some new stories for you." Link and Mary laughed.

Joe smiled and said, "Don't be too cocky. I was talking about you when he dozed off."

Link laughed slightly and approached Kirkland's visible ear. "Just can't take it, huh, Sonnyboy? Not enough real-life drama?" Link laughed again.

He hoisted the shot Joe had poured for him and toasted the one thing he almost never spoke about.

He toasted the one thing that Lucky Jake's always made him think about. He toasted all that mattered to him as he looked into Mary's eyes with as much love as he could.

He took one last look at the shot as he mentioned his one unmentionable thought. He thought about the poetry as he spoke the words, he thought about burning candles, bar stools, and the man in the tuxedo.

"To the price of freedom." He drank quickly and smoothly, and then he slapped Kirkland on the back, rousing him from his sleep. He laughed as Kirkland gurgled. Then he put his arm around Mary and, together, they left.

Joe the bartender drank Link's toast—it was only proper.

Then he poured himself a larger shot and drank it quickly. He couldn't shake the nagging feeling he had, the silent sadness he felt, his intuitive feeling that living poetry may be really neat, but it ain't worth it if no one ever reads the poem.

Kirkland looked around the empty bar in drunken astonishment. "What happened?" said the bleary-eyed junior executive who would undoubtedly be a vice president someday.

"They're all gone, son. Why don't you go home, too, so I can clean up this mess? We'll have a completely different crowd of drunks in here tomorrow."

Song for the Wretched

Father McCarthy slumped in the gold high-backed chair that sat upon the altar. Three fingers of his left hand gently massaged his left temple as his eyes closed and began to tear. For a moment, he held his head and stared at the window of his church. It was such a beautiful day, such a beautiful day. He wiped his left hand across his eyes and nose, and then held it out in front of him, studying the veins as they crossed over the bones. His hand looked old.

He turned his gaze towards the red rug upon the altar. He shook his head slightly and absentmindedly looked back at the red wall-to-wall carpet on the floor. If so many cross this rug, believing it to be the road to salvation, why is the carpet so well preserved? Why is it not worn out in any way? The old priest knew that many were on their way to his church to seek solace in the empty platitudes and clichés that describe misery, suffering, and death. Did this really ease the pain of his parishioners? Did it help them to hear of unspeakable sadness tied to the language of the stupid? Did it make their suffering more meaningful because the words used to describe it had been spoken ten thousand times before? He shook his head again. The tears reappeared in his eyes as he slumped helplessly in his chair.

"My life has been wasted," he thought. "I've not done a meaningful thing or helped anyone truly in need, and that was all I was charged with doing for my entire life. How wasteful, how despicable, how evil I have been."

As the good father evaluated his life, the church doors flew open and a mob of crying people flew in looking for hope and absolution. Women were screaming. Children were frightened. Men wore hollow, vacant looks. The priest's demeanor softened, and he stood on the carpet which was the pathway to redemption, held his hands aloft, and begged for order and quiet from the assembled multitude.

"We don't have much time," he said, in response to the group. "Let us pray now, while we can."

The priest began to pray and order was restored. The people followed him in prayer, hopeful that prayer would help them escape their fate or better prepare them for the way of the Lord.

• • •

Josiah was a woodworker in Hannibal, Vermont. He lived in three small cabins that he had strung together into one some years ago. The place was tiny. He had one small bathroom and electricity enough to light his mountain home and power his woodworking tools. The home had no furnace. Josiah had bought a wood-burning stove some years ago, and it still worked well today. Josiah saw no need to replace something old if it still worked the way it should. Sometimes, he thought it ironic that a woodworker would use a wood-burning stove. It seemed so counterintuitive. He loved wood. He molded, shaped, and formed wood into some incredibly lovely things that he'd shared with family members and friends. But he also loved heat, and winter in his area of Vermont was known to hit thirty below zero. It was on those days that Josiah had a particular affinity for his old wood-burning stove. He'd go outside and his spit would freeze before it hit the ground. He'd come inside and be warm as toast fresh from the toaster. Sometimes, he felt that he straddled two universes: one of wood lovers and the other of wood burners. Other times, he attributed the thought to the addled meanderings brought on by living alone in the Vermont wilderness. A man living with extreme nature in extreme conditions can develop some strange and extreme thoughts.

Josiah's wife had died of pneumonia some fifteen years ago. His daughter left the cabin and Vermont some time after that to go to college and construct her own life. Josiah continued to work with the wood. He built himself a workshop. Over time, he created a lot of beautiful furniture, which he shared with his daughter, her husband, and his friends in the area.

His daughter and his granddaughter came by for visits about three times a year. Her husband sometimes came along, but it was an existence too rugged and remote for him to bear, so he more often stayed away. Josiah paused for a moment and thought about the son-in-law whom he had viewed as weak at times. The boy had died a little over a year ago in a plane crash in New York City. His daughter and granddaughter were crushed by his death. Josiah did what he could to help them, but they were inconsolable. About six months ago, his daughter bought a cabin in a remote part of North Dakota, far away from all reminders of her husband. Although Josiah realized that this was her way of dealing with grief, he had to admit that he found some pleasure in the fact that she had chosen a cabin in a remote spot as a place to build a new life and feel safe again.

The girls were coming to visit Josiah next week, and he was very excited. He was working on a special wooden horse as a gift for his granddaughter, Patti, who loved the ornate horses of the merry-go-round. Josiah was determined to put all of the skill he had accumulated over his lifetime into this horse. Every detail would be perfect and precise. Little Patti would have his best work, so that she could remember her grandpa for the rest of her life.

The detail he placed in the construction of the horse's

head was exquisite. The body was carefully sculpted to highlight the long muscles and great form of a horse born at the dawn of all things. This was a horse suitable for the gods to ride. He wanted his granddaughter to love it and appreciate it. But, most of all, he wanted Patti to keep this horse forever as a remembrance of all the good that lived in her grandfather's heart, a sign of his love for her mother and her mother's mother.

For a moment, his work was interrupted by the sounds of gunshots and screaming from the surrounding mountaintops. He thought the noise odd and disconcerting, but he did not pay it great heed. Though it was early in the day, he assumed that a few of the locals had gotten liquored up and were celebrating some small victory of no consequence. He returned to his project. The girls were due in a week, and he wanted it to be finished when they arrived.

• • •

Tommy Eagan sat in his fifth-floor Manhattan walk-up. There were empty beer bottles, half-full ashtrays, and partially eaten snacks on all of the tables in his apartment save the one on which he was presently working. His book was almost completed. He felt that, with a few more well-crafted pages, he could stitch together the end of his story and declare the work finished. This book was important to Tom. He had spent the better part of two years writing it. To him, it was the key to the sunlight that was his life.

He couldn't wait to publish. Besides, he knew today was his target date to work on the dedication also. He wanted that to be very special.

He stopped working for a moment and stared at the sandstone apartment building that stood across the street from him. Some blinds were up, others were down. His favorite aerobic exerciser had finished her workout and was likely showering. A very fat woman with very large breasts leaned out of her window and watered the plants in her window box. With her thick glasses and slovenly standards of dress, she was always a focus of disdain for Tommy.

His eyes drifted to the street and the usual flow of people who moved like root weevils before him. Tom was never very interested in their existence unless it could be converted into material for his book. As he looked down upon the people below from his fifth-floor perch, he felt, quite literally, above it all.

His glance was captured by a young couple across the way who had just moved out onto their fire escape naked, obviously planning some form of elevated fornication. He wondered how people could be so oblivious to their surroundings. He wondered what motivated them to this public display of their lust. He lit a cigarette, sipped some coffee, and sat back to watch. The finish to his book could wait.

The couple's bodies, now entwined, were beginning

to move at a feverish pace, as Tom watched with extreme interest.

Suddenly church bells started ringing and people flocked onto the sidewalks, screaming. Tom, distracted and alarmed, was trying to hear what everyone was saying. The couple did not pause for a millisecond. They were striving for new levels of climax in the public square.

• • •

Regyl Featherstone was a top prospect for the pros. When asked how high he could jump, his answer was always "as high as I need to," and he would smile the self-assured smile of a top athlete at the height of his game. Regyl had grown up with loud music, alcohol, drugs, and violence surrounding him. He had always wanted something more from life. Basketball was the answer for him. "B-ball is the key to the rain, my brothers," he'd always say. "That money is going to rain down on old Regyl, and Regyl's reign is going to be long and happy."

Regyl embraced the swaggering optimism of youth tempered by a childhood that required him to grow up too fast. The rough streets of the city made him better. Rather than sinking to the lowest common denominator of all that surrounded him, Regyl was motivated to break out and be successful.

Scouts started watching him early. Fast-talking agents in alligator shoes were constantly putting $100 bills in his hands, telling him how much they could do for him.

Everyone recognized Regyl's talent; everyone wanted to get on board and ride to the top with him. "This kid is different," they'd say. "He doesn't live on the street, he learned from the street." Regyl was a good kid.

Regyl soaked up all the attention. He still had vivid memories of hiding in the closet when the screaming began, crying in fear when bottles were hurled at the wall or broken in anger. Sometimes, there was blood. At all times, he felt fear. Determined to get away from everything he ever knew, Regyl saw his talent as the deliverer of happiness and great fortune.

A couple of his friends knocked on his door. He would go down to the schoolyard to play once more. As they left his building, Regyl and his friends heard sounds of shouting and crying coming from the apartments. The streets were a mass of confusion: Mothers were wailing, children were screaming, people were running in every direction. Regyl looked around in a state of bemused fascination. He thought the hood was a bit madder than usual today, and all the noise brought a cynical smile to his face. The noise was cacophonous, the sounds a jumbled mass of the inscrutable and indecipherable. Other friends yelled to Regyl, but he could not hear them above the din.

• • •

Jim Phat ate bologna sandwiches in the park. Jim was a Taiwanese hobo, which made him unique in his community. He had a fake monkey draped over his shoulder. This was his begging prop. He called the monkey Mr. Chimps, and he loved the monkey more than anything else in the world.

Jim's friends had left him some time ago. Most left shortly after he lost all his money in a gambling disaster about which he rarely spoke. His wife tried to stab him on three separate occasions. His kids hated him because he had lost what little joy in life they had.

Jim remembered what it was like to be normal because he realized how empty his life felt now that he was alone. His loneliness fed his sense of desperation and hopelessness. He fell deeper into a life of what he called meaningless isolation.

Losing was something Jim did well. He prided himself on losing with class. Some felt that this was the reason he lost so often—Jim Phat was dying to show the world how classy he was.

Anyway, Phat was "tap city" now, sitting cross-legged in Madison Square Park watching while little kids played on a nearby swing set. Phat had a "Phunny" way about him, and any who paid any attention at all to the odd things he said appreciated his offbeat take on the world of the living. It had been such a long time since he had felt like he was a part of that world: Sometimes his jokes and phunny observations made little sense to him. He felt like he was a character in an uninteresting play, and he did not know how it would end or what role he played in it.

In a moment that living alone had caused Phat to appreciate, he watched with fascination as a very large rat chased and treed a squirrel. The squirrel was quaking in fear, certain that the presence of this rat had meant the end of him. His amusement was interrupted by loud screams and people running onto the streets in what seemed to be a panic.

• • •

A man walked alone in the tall grass prairie in northeast Oklahoma. He gazed into what seemed to be the everlasting distance, looking for signs of the last of the free-range bison. He saw a couple of hundred once, not so long ago. He'd not seen any since. The wind was strong and steady, the air hot, but not stifling. The trees rustled as the sun danced between some flimsy cumulus clouds. In the shade beside a stream, he felt the infinite stillness of nature. He felt that Nature, in the swaying of the trees and the movement of the sun between the clouds and among the leaves, was imparting a message to which he must attend. There was not a human being within fifteen miles of where he stood. The isolation moved his mind to meditation. The constant wind now whipping his face made him believe that he was looking into the eyes of God.

Two crows (or were they hawks?) pierced the sky before him. There was a sudden shift in the wind, and the trees seemed to shudder and crack. He thought that he saw a series of bright flashes in the east, and irrational fear overtook him. He felt an urgent need to leave the prairie and drive toward town. There was the date with Mary tonight and the ride to Grand Lake tomorrow.

• • •

The priest held his hands aloft, "We must pray. There is not much time." The church was filled now with worshippers deep in prayer, quietly crying, or screaming in panic. "We must pray," said the priest again, and his voice trailed off. He realized that no one was listening.

• • •

Josiah never finished the horse for his granddaughter.

Tommy Eagan never finished his book.

Regyl didn't believe a word anyone said. He thought it was all a joke. He thought they were all crazy. A bright white light flashed as his shot flew into the air.

Jim Phat never ate bologna again, and he didn't see the squirrel survive his bout with the rat.

The man from the high grass prairie was dead before he got to Tulsa.

• • •

They say that there is nothing worse than aging, no lonelier feeling than the slow and inevitable realization that your body can't do what it once did. Your mind can't function as well as it once did, and your friends begin to die, one at a time, for no apparent reason.

Then, there is the alternative.